AF393616

Druck und Distribution im Auftrag der Autorin:

tredition GmbH, Heinz-Beusen-Stieg 5, 22926 Ahrensburg, Deutschland

L.H. Kuhrau

Author from the well-known book series

One last...

Beat

Death

Suffer-ring

Mistake

A
First
Mistake

A first...

Beat

Death

Suffer-ring

Mistake

Chapter 1

I have to run.

They are so close behind me, I can almost hear their breathing or feel it in my neck.

I have to run faster.

Never had I been the one who had to escape. Never did I have to run away. I was just used to killing and using all my power against everybody, which wasn't likeable for me. Now, as I got away from my old mafia life, it was me who had to run away. It was nobody else but me; they wanted to see dead.

Suddenly I hear a shot behind me.

They wouldn't just shoot me. That would be all too easy. All too soft. From their side, I would surely have to deserve the most painful. I would be subjected to torture for several days or even weeks. I was forced to eat my own food while they were enjoying the most delicious dinners in front of me.

It had been my choice. I wanted to run away. I wanted to come away from that life. Never had I chosen it. I never desired it, nor had I anticipated waking up as the future leader. My sole desire as a leader was to witness his demise. Carlo. Carlo is the man who stole everything from me. He was the one who snatched her away.

Another scream. "He is here." I nearly fell to the ground, but I managed to hide behind a large tree before the knife could have hidden me.

Since then, have we returned to the eighteenth century and resumed our knife-wielding activities? What has transpired since my departure from that society?

As I look beside me, I see the knife just an inch away from my head. I take a last deep breath before I want to continue my run.

I have no chance.

Before I can start to move my leg, they have surrounded me already. This is the final stage; I am about to meet my demise.

I woke up covered with sweat. I detest the persistent nightmare that haunts me every time I fall asleep or even close my eyes for more than a moment. I want to be free. I never chose the life I was forced to lead because my father had joined the mafia. Carlo had taught me everything, but that didn't mean I was prepared to sacrifice my life to become the leader of hell.

However, as the sun hits my face, everything is forgotten. I am here, miles away from anything hidden in the forest. The morning sun serves as a constant reminder of this fact and invigorates my spirit. I ran away for a reason; even though Lena is no longer alive, following her plan feels like being with her again.

Of course, I still miss her, but at least I have the freedom to pursue our shared interests now. This doesn't entail eliminating all those who deceived me, as I did prior to departing from my family; instead, I have discovered tranquillity in this place.

At least almost. If I fell asleep and experienced nightmares, I would undoubtedly forget about the peaceful place I had reached for a while.

As I stand up, I stretch myself and start my usual morning routine with the training. Even if I am no longer in the mafia, I still have to stay in shape and be ready for a dispute once it happens. At once, as they find me.

After my sessions I want to get some food, but as I get on my way I hear something.

Even if I have some animal neighbours, there are usually no people here. Through I would survive seeing some from the normal world, it would be painful enough to just know that any mafia person enters my safe space here on the mountain.

Again. I hear it louder this time. That isn't good. There are two options: either I approach the producer more closely, or they approach me directly. Whatever the situation, I must distance myself from it. There is no way the delivery services noticed that I was hungry. That person isn't here to help me. Perhaps they have a deeper desire to see me die...

Chapter 2

I've always wondered what it could have been—the life that I never got to live. The one without blood. Without betrayal. Every decision I make tugs me towards something more sinister. But as much as I try to push it away, it always feels like there's something inside me, clawing its way back to the surface. That's the thing; you can leave the war, but it never leaves you.

I've been walking for hours, far away from where I started. The sun is just beginning to rise, casting a hazy orange glow over the horizon. The air smells fresh, like dew and pine needles. My clothes are still damp from the river crossing earlier, and every now and then, I stop to wring out the fabric between my hands, watching the water drip and disappear into the dirt.

However, it doesn't bother me. Nothing does, really—not anymore. Because this... this is my reality now. Alone. Every step further away from the life I once knew is another step into the unknown. Into whatever it could be. However, despite my best efforts to convince myself that I've moved on, the shadow persists. The darkness persists, tugging me back.

The only thing keeping me from diving headfirst into despair is the routine. I take one step at a time, take one breath, and cherish each moment of solitude. It's how I survive.

I come across a small clearing, the forest opening up to reveal a river, slow-moving and clear. The water reflects the sky above, an endless canvas of blue stretching over me. I crouch by the riverbank, letting my fingers dip into the cool water. For a moment, I close my eyes, feeling the pull of the current against my hand. It reminds me of how life flows. Steady, unstoppable. But no matter how much it flows forward, there's always that undercurrent of danger lurking beneath the surface.

I shake the thought off and splash the water against my face. It feels good, refreshing. I breathe in and inhale the clean air. It's the little things, like this—the quiet moments that remind me I'm still human and that I'm not just a product of my past. But the quiet never lasts long. The ghosts always find a way to creep back in.

As I stand, I hear something rustling in the bushes nearby. My instincts kick in—years of training, years of surviving. I freeze, listening closely, every muscle tensing as I slowly turn toward the noise. The bushes rustle again, and my hand automatically moves toward my side, even though I have no weapon anymore. I left that life behind. Or so I thought.

For a brief moment, I find myself back in the midst of the chaos, anticipating the impending ambush and the inevitable betrayal. My breath quickens, and my pulse pounds in my ears. But then a shape emerges from the brush. Not a person. Not an enemy. Just a dog.

He is a mutt, scrawny and slender, possessing matted fur and eyes that appear to have endured a significant amount of hardship. He stares at me from a distance, his head cocked to the side, as if he's sizing me up the same way I'm sizing him. For a moment, we just stand there, staring at each other, neither of us making a move.

Then, slowly, cautiously, the dog takes a step forward, sniffing the air between us. I relax just a little, letting my hand fall to my side. He's no threat. Like me, he's just trying to survive.

"Hey there," I say quietly, my voice rough from disuse. The dog stops, watching me closely. I reach into my pocket and pull out a small piece of dried meat—something I'd kept from earlier when I raided a small store for supplies. I hold it out to him, and after a moment of hesitation, the dog moves closer, his nose twitching as he sniffs the offering.

He takes the meat from my hand gently, his eyes never leaving mine. There's a cautious trust there, a mutual understanding between two creatures who have been through hell and back. I crouch down, letting him get used to my presence.

"You've been through it too, haven't you?" I murmur, running my hand gently over his back. His fur is rough, tangled with dirt and leaves, but he doesn't pull away. In fact, he leans into my touch, as if he's been starved for affection for far too long.

I watch him devour the piece of meat, his hunger evident in the way he gulps it down in seconds. I pull out another piece and give it to him, watching as he eats, more at ease now.

"What should I call you?" I inquire, not fully anticipating a response. He looks up at me, his dark eyes filled with something I can't quite place.

"Shoot," I say finally. "You look like a good Shoot."

The dog seems to approve. He doesn't bark, doesn't wag his tail, but there's something in the way he stays close, watching me with those knowing eyes, that tells me he understands.

We sit in silence for a while, the only sound being the gentle lapping of the river and the occasional rustle of the leaves in the breeze. Shoot lies down beside me, his body pressing against my leg as if he's made his choice. He's chosen to trust me for now.

I feel a strange sense of comfort in his presence. It's been a long time since I've felt that way. Too long.

I take off my shoes and step into the river, the cold water rushing over my feet. It feels good, cleansing in a way I didn't know I needed. I walk a little deeper, until the water is up to my knees, letting the current tug at me. It's peaceful here. Too peaceful.

And that's when it happens.

A scream. Faint, but unmistakable. It cuts through the quiet like a knife, sending a jolt of adrenaline through my body. I freeze, listening, my mind racing. It's distant, but close enough to know it's real. Not some figment of my imagination.

Shoot is on his feet instantly; his ears perked up, his body tense. He looks at me, waiting for my reaction, but I'm frozen in place, torn between two worlds.

Everything, including the blood, violence, and betrayals, suddenly resurfaces. Every sound, every scream—every moment of my past comes crashing down on me like a wave, threatening to pull me under. My breath comes in short, sharp bursts, and I clench my fists, trying to steady myself.

I thought I could escape it. I thought I could leave it all behind. But as much as I want to, it's always there, lurking just beneath the surface, waiting for the right moment to drag me back in.

The scream echoes again, louder this time, more desperate. I grit my teeth, forcing myself to move, breathe, and think.

It's not my problem. It's not my fight anymore. I came here to get away from all that and to start over. To be something—someone—different. But no matter how hard I try, it's never that simple.

Shoot whines beside me, nudging my leg with his nose, as if urging me to do something. Anything.

I take a deep breath, closing my eyes for a brief moment. The river flows around me, steady and constant. But even in this peaceful place, the darkness finds a way in.

When I open my eyes again, I make my decision.

I step out of the river, my feet sinking into the muddy bank as I reach for my shoes. Shoot watches me closely, sensing the change in me, the shift in my resolve. I slip on my shoes, not bothering to tie them, and turn toward the direction of the scream.

This isn't my fight. But I can't ignore it. Not anymore.

I start walking, my steps steady, determined. Shoot follows close behind, his silent presence a reminder that I'm not alone. Maybe, just maybe, there's still a part of me that can't turn away from a fight. No matter how much I want to, there's a part of me that can't let go.

As we move deeper into the forest, the scream fades into the distance, swallowed by the trees and the wind. But the memory of it lingers, hanging in the air like a ghost. No matter how far I run, I can't escape who I am. What I've always been.

A survivor. A fighter. A man haunted by his own darkness.

And as much as I want to believe that I can be something else—someone else—I know the truth.

The shadows will always follow me. No matter where I go, no matter how far I run, they'll always be there. Waiting.

Just like they are now.

Chapter 3

The scream echoed through the trees, still lingering in the cool morning air. My pulse thundered in my ears, each beat a reminder of where I'd come from. What I'd left behind. But I was here now, far away from the city, from the life that had marked me so deeply.

I forced myself to keep walking. Step after step. Don't look back. Just keep moving. It wasn't my problem. Not anymore. I wasn't that man anymore—the one who answered screams, who ran toward danger. That life was over. I had to believe that. I had to.

The sound of footsteps crunched on the leaves behind me—steady, determined. Shoot followed closely, his pace matching mine, but with every step, I felt a sharp stab of frustration. His presence was a reminder of the connection I didn't want, the obligation I never asked for. He padded along quietly, but even the faintest sound of his paws on the groundgnawed at my nerves. I tried to push it out of my mind, but the anger simmered below the surface, threatening to break through.

I clenched my fists, my jaw tightening with every passing second. Why couldn't he just leave me alone? Why did he have to follow me—trailing behind like a shadow I couldn't shake?

"Stop following me," I muttered under my breath, knowing full well that the dog wouldn't understand. But the footsteps continued—persistent and unwavering. My anger flared again, and before I could stop myself, I spun around, glaring at him.

"Stop!" I shouted, my voice harsher than I intended.

Shoot froze in his tracks, his eyes wide, his body stiff. He didn't move; he didn't make a sound. He just stood there, staring at me with those same dark, knowing eyes.

For a moment, I felt a flicker of guilt, but it was quickly buried under the weight of my anger. I couldn't afford to care. Not now. Not ever.

I turned back around, determined to keep moving—to keep running. That was all I knew how to do. I had to disappear again, to fade into the background like a ghost. I had to survive.

However, just a few seconds later then another sound reached my ears. This time, it wasn't a scream. It was softer, weaker. A plea.

"Help..."

The word halted me abruptly, cutting through the barrier I had constructed around myself. My heart pounded in my chest, and I clenched my fists again, trying to block it out. I couldn't turn back. I couldn't get involved.

The voice echoed in my mind, twisting something inside me. I hated myself for it. For that moment of hesitation. I long for the glimmer of humanity that I thought I had long since buried.

I stepped forward, then stopped. My breath came in shallow, ragged bursts. Every fiber of my being screamed at me to move, to run—to forget I'd ever heard it. But my feet wouldn't budge.

I squeezed my eyes shut, cursing under my breath.

Why couldn't I just leave? Why couldn't I just walk away?

Because you're still that man.

As I opened my eyes, the realization struck me with a forceful jolt. No matter how far I ran, no matter how much I tried to escape, I was still that man. I was unable to turn away or walk away. And I hated it. I hated myself for it.

The voice came again, weaker this time.

"Help... please."

I swallowed hard, my throat tight. I couldn't do this. I shouldn't do this.

However, I couldn't stop myself. Slowly, reluctantly, I turned toward the sound, my heart pounding in my chest. Shoot was already ahead of me, his nose to the ground as if he knew where we were headed.

I followed him, my steps heavy, each one feeling like a betrayal of the life I was trying to leave behind. The closer I got, the more my mind raced. What if it was a trap? What if someone was waiting for me? What if I was walking straight into another nightmare?

And then... then I saw her.

She was wedged between two rocks, her body twisted in a way that made my own limbs ache just from looking at her. Her leg was caught in a narrow crack, her ankle swollen and bruised. She couldn't have been more than twenty, with long, dark hair that clung to her tear-streaked face. Her eyes were wide with pain, but when they locked on mine, they were filled with something else.

Desperation.

I stood there, frozen, staring at her. This wasn't my problem. I wasn't supposed to be here. I wasn't supposed to care.

But I did.

She let out a weak sob, her body trembling as she tried to pull herself free. But it was no use. She was stuck.

I should've walked away. I should've turned my back and kept going. But I didn't.

"Please," she whispered, her voice barely audible. "Help me."

I let out a slow breath, my mind racing. If I helped her, I risked everything. Getting involved meant being seen. It meant being part of the world again. It meant I couldn't disappear the way I needed to.

But if I left her here...

I shook my head, trying to clear my thoughts. This wasn't supposed to happen. I wasn't supposed to care. But the sight of her—helpless, broken, trapped—pulled at something deep inside me. I believed I had buried it long ago.

Slowly, I took a step forward. Then another.

Shoot followed closely behind, his eyes never leaving mine. He didn't make a sound, but I could feel his presence, steady and reassuring.

When I reached her, I crouched down, my heart pounding in my chest. She looked up at me, her eyes filled with pain and fear, but there was something else there too. Hope.

"I'll get you out," I said quietly, my voice barely a whisper.

Her eyes widened, and she nodded weakly, tears streaming down her face. I reached for her leg, gently touching the area where it was caught between the rocks. She winced, sucking in a sharp breath, but she didn't pull away.

"Stay still," I said, my voice soft but firm. "I need to check how bad it is."

She nodded again, biting down on her lip as I carefully examined her leg. The ankle was twisted at an awkward angle, clearly broken, but the rest of her seemed unharmed. If I could just free her...

"I'm going to lift the rock," I said, glancing at her. "When I do, I need you to pull your leg out. Can you do that?"

She nodded, her face pale, her breathing shallow.

I took a deep breath, bracing myself. The rock wasn't huge, but it was wedged tightly against the other one. It would take all my strength to move it.

"On three," I said, positioning myself.

"One..."

"Two…"

I heaved with everything I had, my muscles straining as I lifted the rock just enough for her to pull her leg free. She let out a cry of pain, but she didn't hesitate. She yanked her leg out, collapsing onto the ground the moment she was free.

I dropped the rock, breathing heavily, my arms trembling from the effort. Shoot was by her side in an instant, sniffing at her leg, his nose twitching as if he could sense the pain.

She lay there for a moment, panting, her face contorted in agony. But then, slowly, she opened her eyes and looked at me.

"Thank you," she whispered, her voice hoarse. "Thank you."

I nodded, unable to find the words. The reality of what I'd done was sinking in. I'd helped her. I'd saved her.

Now, I had a choice to make.

I could leave her here. I could walk away, disappear again, and let her deal with the consequences. Or I could stay. I could help her, make sure she was safe, and make sure she survived.

But if I stayed… if I helped her…

I'd be putting myself at risk. I'd be exposing myself. I'd be dragging myself back into the world I'd fought so hard to leave behind.

I looked at her, lying there, helpless and broken, and I felt that familiar pull. That urge to protect. To save. To do the right thing.

However, following the correct path was what initially led me into this predicament.

I stood up, my mind racing.

What was I supposed to do?

Chapter 4

Silas watched her, her leg still throbbing with pain, and her face pale and damp with sweat. The reality of the situation sank in deeper now, like a weight in his chest. He hadn't just freed her from the rocks. He'd crossed a line—a line he swore he wouldn't touch ever again. Yet, here he was, standing over her, the strange mix of guilt and determination twisting through his veins.

"Can you stand?" His voice was low, neutral.

The young woman looked up at him, biting her lip as she nodded. She braced herself against the cold ground, her arms trembling as she tried to push herself up. Her broken ankle gave way beneath her, and she winced, her breath catching in her throat as she collapsed back onto the earth.

Silas cursed under his breath. "You can't make it alone. I'll help you."

Her eyes met his, wide and uncertain. "But..."

However, she couldn't finish the sentence. She didn't know who he was, why he was here, or why a man like him would even bother to stop and help. It was as if she could sense that he didn't belong. He was no longer doing this for people like her.

Without another word, Silas crouched beside her, slipping his arm under her shoulders and hoisting her up gently. She gasped, the pain seeping through every movement, but she didn't resist. Her body sagged against his, too exhausted to fight the help she desperately needed.

"Lean on me," Silas muttered. "You've got no other choice."

Her weight was nothing compared to the heaviness he felt inside. As he guided her slowly through the thick trees, each step pushing them closer to the edge of the forest, Silas's mind raced. His hands felt the warmth of her body, but he could already feel the cold creep back in—the cold of the isolation he'd been running toward, the darkness he craved.

They stumbled forward in silence, her breaths ragged, his measured and distant. Each step felt like a betrayal to the life he had built for himself, the exile he had accepted. The shadows around him whispered, reminding him that he didn't belong in the world of the living anymore—not in the world of saving anyone.

Minutes bled into an hour. He could now see the road through the thinning trees. Civilization. Safety for her, danger for him.

He felt the tension growing inside him, his skin crawling the closer they got. He was inches away from being seen. Being known. His instincts screamed at him to turn back, to run, to leave her to fate.

They reached the edge of the forest. The road stretched ahead, a ribbon of asphalt cutting through the wilderness. Empty. Silent.

Silas let go of her, his body stiff as he helped her sit by the road, propping her up against a nearby rock. Her face was ghostly pale, but there was a spark of relief in her eyes. She had made it.

Silas looked down at her, his throat tightening. He wanted to leave, to disappear into the woods again without a second thought. He couldn't afford to stay here any longer. His pulse raced, and his gaze darted toward the distant trees.

"You did this alone," Silas said gruffly. His voice was cold and detached, but his heart pounded in his chest. "Nobody helped you."

She blinked at him, confusion washing over her features. "But..."

"Forget me." His voice was firm now. "Forget everything. When someone finds you, you tell them you made it here on your own. That no one was there."

She stared at him, wide-eyed, her lips parting as if to protest, but the words caught in her throat. Instead, she swallowed hard, nodding slowly. The pain in her leg was no match for the mystery of the man standing in front of her. His sharp edges and haunting eyes left her wondering who he was and why he was running.

Silas turned, stepping away from her, his body rigid, ready to vanish into the forest once more. But just as his foot hit the edge of the tree line, her voice called after him, soft and broken.

"Thank you," she whispered. "Nobody..."

Silas paused, his back to her, his jaw clenched tight. He didn't turn around. He couldn't. The weight of her gratitude—her acknowledgement—was suffocating. He didn't deserve it.

"Maybe we'll meet twice in life," she added softly, the words barely reaching him.

A bitter laugh almost escaped his lips. Twice in life? Maybe in a different world. Maybe at a different time. But not in this one. Not for someone like him.

Without another word, Silas pushed forward into the shadows, leaving her behind. The further he went, the heavier his chest became. His breath quickened, his muscles tensing as the familiar rhythm of the forest began to swallow him up again. The gentle crunch of leaves beneath his boots and the sound of wind rustling through the trees evoked a sense of familiarity. So safe. Yet every step he took felt hollow.

Shoot followed silently, his eyes never leaving Silas, but the dog's presence only intensified the weight pressing on him. It was meant to stay that way after so long alone. But now? Now the universe was playing tricks on him, throwing obstacles in his path. Making him feel things again.

He walked for miles, putting as much distance between himself and the road as possible. The deeper he went into the woods, the darker it became, the air thick with silence. His chest tightened with every breath he took, his heart racing as the memories began to claw their way back into his mind.

The scream. The blood. He stared at the faces of those he had abandoned. He squeezed his eyes shut, trying to force them away, but they wouldn't leave him. They never did.

His legs ached, his body screamed for rest, but he kept pushing forward, kept running. Maybe if he ran far enough—fast enough— he could outrun it all. He was overcome by the memories, the guilt, and the person he once was.

Still, he knew the truth. No matter how far he ran—no matter how deep into the forest he disappeared—it would never be enough.

Finally, after what felt like hours, Silas stopped. His body gave in to exhaustion; his legs trembled as he fell to his knees in the dirt. He's far enough now. He was sufficiently distanced so that no one could track him. He could vanish once more from sight.

Shoot sat beside him, his eyes watching, waiting. But Silas didn't acknowledge him. He couldn't. He was too tired. Too broken.

He glanced up at the sky, the stars twinkling faintly through the gaps in the trees. The night was cold, but it didn't bother him. He barely felt it.

A part of him wanted to lie down, to close his eyes, and never wake up. He wanted to surrender to the forest, surrender to the darkness. Maybe that was the only way out. The only way to truly escape.

He closed his eyes, his breath shallow, his body heavy with exhaustion. His mind began to drift, the weight of everything pulling him deeper and deeper into the abyss.

However, as much as he wanted to let go and disappear, there was still something inside him. He clung to life despite his reluctance.

The forest was quiet now; the only sound was the soft rustle of leaves in the wind. Silas lay down on the cold earth, his body curling in on itself. He didn't know if he would wake up. He didn't know if he wanted to.

All he knew was that, for the first time in a long time, he felt scared. He was not afraid of the outside world or the individuals who might be searching for him.

He was scared of himself. Of the man he had become. Of the men he could never outrun.

The darkness closed in around him, and he let it. He allowed the darkness to embrace him, even if it was only for a brief moment. Perhaps, in the tranquility of the forest, he might discover the tranquility he'd been seeking. He had been searching for this peace for an extended period.

But deep down, he knew the truth.

Peace wasn't something that came to men like him.

It wasn't something you found.

It was something you lost.

And Silas... had already lost everything.

Chapter 5

The cold morning air pressed down on me as I lay still, eyes closed, trying to claw my way back to sleep, but something felt wrong. My body was tense, as though it had sensed danger before my mind could even catch up. The forest around me was too quiet. There were no birds or rustling leaves, only an unsettling silence that indicated something was amiss. And then I felt it—a sharp pressure against the side of my head.

Instinct kicked in. My eyes snapped open, and there it was. A gun. Cold metal pressed hard against my temple. My gaze followed the weapon to the man gripping it, and I froze.

Martin.

The bastard stood over me, his eyes hard, his face weathered with lines that told a story of desperation, anger, and determination. Of all the people I thought would find me, I hadn't expected Martin. Not him.

"Finally," he muttered under his breath, his voice rough. "Thought I'd never track you down."

My pulse quickened, but I forced myself to stay calm. I'd gotten out of worse. Much worse.

Shoot was beside me, curled up near my feet. The dog hadn't sensed the danger yet—or maybe he had, but hadn't moved. He was smarter than most gave him credit for.

I waited for the right moment. It was a delicate balance—if I twitched too soon, Martin would put a bullet through my skull. If I hesitated too long, my chance to take control would slip away.

Then I saw it—the flicker of uncertainty in Martin's eyes, just a brief hesitation. He wasn't sure. He didn't have the same cold resolve as Carlo. Carlo wouldn't have hesitated. He'd have pulled the trigger without thinking twice. But Martin? He wanted something from me.

"Shoot!" I clearly and loudly delivered the command.

Martin's eyes widened in panic. For a brief moment, he believed that he was not alone. He anticipated a team, backup, or someone approaching from behind to overpower him. Instinct took over. He turned, the barrel of the gun swinging away from me as he braced himself for a fight. But there was no one else.

Just Shoot.

The dog lunged forward, teeth bare, sinking into Martin's leg with a ferocity that took him by surprise. Martin screamed, his grip on the gun loosening as he stumbled, trying to shake off the dog. Between his leg pain and panic, he was distracted. And that's all I needed.

I rolled to my feet in one smooth motion, grabbing a thick branch beside me and swinging it with all the force I could muster. The wood connected with Martin's head, and he crumpled to the ground, unconscious, before he even hit the dirt.

Panting, I stood over him, my hands shaking. I looked down at Shoot, who was still growling, his teeth buried in Martin's leg.

"Easy, boy," I whispered, pulling the dog away. "We got him."

Shoot released Martin's leg, licking the blood from his muzzle before sitting obediently at my feet. His eyes were locked on me, waiting for the next command. I gave him a nod of approval and turned my attention back to the unconscious man before me.

Martin had found me. Martin had somehow managed to locate me after all this time.

I dragged his limp body over to a nearby tree and worked quickly, using rope from my pack to bind his hands and feet. I checked his pockets, tossing aside anything that could be used as a weapon or a signal to whoever else might be looking for me. Once he was securely tied up, I took a deep breath and tried to calm the storm raging inside me.

Shoot sat nearby, his tail wagging slowly, as if he had just completed a simple task. He had no idea what he'd just helped me avoid. Martin's success would have resulted in our deaths by now.

I glanced at the sky, the morning sun barely breaking through the thick canopy of trees above. I had run for years, hoping to leave this life behind. But here it was, chasing me down like it always did. No matter how far I went, the past found a way to drag me back in.

Martin began to stir, his groans muffled by the dirt and leaves beneath him. I glanced over at him as he slowly came to, his eyes fluttering open. It took him a moment to realize where he was and the position he was in—bound to a tree, weaponless, and at my mercy.

"Shit," he muttered, his voice hoarse. He struggled against the ropes, his face twisting with frustration when he realized they weren't coming loose.

I stood up, dusting the dirt from my hands, and walked over to where I had been sitting. Without giving Martin a second glance, I started building a small fire, gathering the dry twigs and leaves around me. My hands moved automatically; the motions were muscle memory at this point. I wasn't thinking about the fire. My mind was elsewhere.

"Silas…" Martin began, his voice weak but laced with bitterness. "You've got no idea how much trouble you're in."

I said nothing, simply focusing on the task in front of me. The fire sparked to life, the flames crackling softly. I pulled a small pan from my bag and set it over the fire, dropping in some of the meager rations I had left.

"I wasn't expecting to be found this soon," I said finally, breaking the silence. "But here you are. How'd you manage that, Martin?"

He let out a humourless laugh. "You think I just stumbled across you? This wasn't a damn accident."

I glanced over at him, my gaze hard. "Then tell me."

Martin's face twisted into a grimace. "You took everything from us. From the family. Now that Carlo is gone, the family is in a chaotic state. The men—they don't know what to do. They need a leader."

I shook my head. "Not my problem anymore."

He laughed again, but it was tinged with bitterness and resentment. "Not your problem? You think you can just walk away from it all? From what you did?" He struggled against the ropes again, his voice rising with frustration. "Carlo's dead because of you. And now the only people left who could lead? They'll tear the family apart in a matter of days."

I stared at him, my mind racing. The family. The old life. I wanted nothing to do with any of it. I had walked away for a reason.

"And why do you care?" I asked, my voice calm, though my insides churned with unease. "Why are you here?"

Martin's eyes narrowed. "Because without you, everything we built will be destroyed."

I could hear the desperation in his voice. He wasn't here for revenge. He wasn't here out of loyalty to Carlo or to take me down. He was here primarily out of fear. He feared the potential consequences of someone else seizing the family's leadership. Someone worse than me.

I turned back to the fire, flipping the food in the pan. "I'm done with all of that, Martin. I left for a reason."

"You left us to die!" he spat, his voice full of anger now. "You walked away from everything. From all of us."

My chest tightened, but I didn't respond. I didn't need to. Martin's words hung in the air like a weight, pressing down on me. I had left. And I hadn't looked back. Not once.

But now, here he was. He pulled me back to a world I had devoted years to erasing.

"How did you find me?" I asked, my voice quieter now, almost a whisper.

Martin's mouth twisted into a grim smile. "She told us."

I froze. My breath caught in my throat as his words sunk in. She told them.

"The girl," Martin continued. "The one you helped. She led us right to you."

The crackling of the fire was the only sound for a long moment. The girl. The one I had pulled from the rocks was broken and helpless. I had saved her life, and in return, she had sold me out.

I clenched my fists, feeling the sharp sting of betrayal. Of course. Of course, this is what happens when you try to help. Stepping out of the shadows allows someone else to briefly enter your life.

"You shouldn't have done it, Silas," Martin said, shaking his head. "You can't just turn your back on the family. On everything we are. You can't run forever."

I felt my chest tighten. Run forever. The truth in those words gnawed at me. Maybe I couldn't. Maybe no matter how far I went or how deep into the wilderness I buried myself, the past would always find me.

However, I wasn't about to let them pull me back in. I had made my own decisions, and they were no longer on my path. Not anymore.

"You're wasting your breath, Martin," I said coldly. "I'm not coming back."

Martin's eyes flared with anger, his body straining against the ropes. "If you don't come back, everything falls apart!" he growled. "And then what? You think you can just hide out here while the family burns? While the world you built crumbles."

I walked over to him, crouching down so we were eye level. His breath was ragged, his face flushed with rage and desperation.

"I didn't build that world," I said, my voice low and steady. "Carlo did. And now he's gone. So let it burn."

Martin's eyes widened; a flicker of fear crossed his face as he realized I wasn't bluffing. I wasn't going to save them. I wasn't going back. I wasn't their solution.

I stood up, walked back toward the fire, picked up the pan, and began eating in silence. Martin sat there, bound and helpless, staring at me with a mixture of disbelief and hatred.

"You're making a mistake," he muttered, his voice trembling.

I didn't respond. There was nothing left to say.

Chapter 6

The sky was a blanket of steel grey when I finally stopped running. My breath came in short, sharp gasps, the muscles in my legs burning from the endless miles I'd covered. I had been running all night, trying to escape the echo of Martin's words, but the truth clung to me, weighing down every step.

"You took everything from us. They cannot be without a leader."

Leader. That word felt foreign now, like a language I had forgotten how to speak. I leaned against a tree, trying to catch my breath, but no amount of air could fill the gaping hole that was my chest.

Shoot padded up beside me, his dark eyes watching me silently. He knew. Hell, the dog probably understood better than I did. I wasn't just running away from the forest, or the girl, or the family. I was running from myself. But no matter how fast or far I went, I couldn't outrun the truth.

My family was dying. The city was on fire, and I wasn't there to stop it.

I closed my eyes, pressing my back harder into the bark. The memories came flooding back—the endless nights spent in that house, learning the game, pulling strings, climbing the ladder of power. I had been at the top once, and now I was just a ghost walking in the shadows, pretending like I didn't belong to the life I had bled for.

The forest felt too silent now, too still. The forest seemed to hold its breath, anticipating my decision, which I had been delaying for an extended period.

"Goddammit." My voice was hoarse, barely more than a whisper, as if saying it out loud would make the decision real.

Deep down, I understood my responsibilities. I had always known. The world I came from—the family—wasn't something you could leave behind. It wasn't something you could escape. It followed you like a shadow—always just out of reach, always waiting for you to come back. And now it was waiting for me.

I couldn't keep running. Not anymore.

With a deep breath, I pushed off the tree and started walking, the weight of my decision heavy in my chest. Shoot followed without a sound, his paws crunching softly in the underbrush. I didn't have a destination in mind, but I knew the direction. The pull of home was too strong to ignore now.

As much as I had tried to be free of it, I was bound to that world. Carlo was aware of this, even though I wasn't. You didn't just walk away from power like that. I could leave the house, the city, the men—but I couldn't leave what had been drilled into my bones since the day I was born.

You took everything from us.

The words echoed in my mind, relentless, a constant reminder of what I had done. I had stripped them of a leader, a structure, and a future. I had been selfish, thinking I could walk away from the responsibility. But now, as I walked through the forest—miles from the chaos of the city—I realized that leaving had been the real betrayal.

I hadn't just abandoned the family. I had abandoned myself.

Hours passed in a blur of trees and dirt paths, my mind too clouded with guilt to notice the landscape shifting around me. By the time I reached the edge of the city, the sky was a dull shade of morning grey, and the streets were just beginning to stir.

It felt strange being back here after so long, like stepping into a world I had once known but no longer recognized. The buildings loomed taller, the streets narrower, and everything felt more suffocating than it had before. I pulled the hood of my jacket lower, my eyes scanning the empty streets for any signs of danger. I couldn't afford to be seen. Not yet.

The warehouse district wasn't far, just a few blocks away. I kept to the shadows, my heart pounding with every step as the memories clawed at me. The faces of the men I had left behind, the ones who had trusted me, flashed through my mind. I could almost hear their voices, their laughter, and the weight of their loyalty.

I left them all to die.

I had been selfish, trying to escape the world I had built, and now I was returning to find the wreckage of what I had abandoned. The realization struck me deeply, yet I continued to walk. I didn't have a choice anymore.

By the time I reached the old warehouse, my chest was tight with anxiety, and my pulse was a steady thrum in my ears. The door was already open, a sliver of light cutting through the darkness, and I slipped inside without a sound.

The room smelt of oil and metal, the familiar scent sending a rush of memories through me. The men were there, scattered around the room in small groups, talking in low voices, their faces heavy with the weight of the past few months.

The conversations ceased as soon as they noticed me.

Silence fell over the room like a heavy curtain, and all eyes turned toward me. For a moment, no one moved. No one spoke. They just stared at me, their eyes wide with a mixture of shock, anger, and disbelief.

Luka was the first to stand. His broad shoulders were tense, his jaw clenched as he stepped toward me. His eyes were dark, filled with a storm of emotions I wasn't sure I wanted to face.

"Silas." His voice was low, almost a growl, as if he were holding back the tide of anger threatening to spill over. "What the hell are you doing here?"

I held his gaze, my heart pounding in my chest. "I came back."

The words hung in the air, heavy and uncertain. They didn't carry the weight of a leader. Not yet.

Luka's fists clenched at his sides, his knuckles white. "You left us. You left us to fend for ourselves, and now you come back like nothing happened? Like we're just supposed to follow you again?"

I swallowed the lump in my throat, forcing myself to keep my voice steady. "I didn't come back to ask for forgiveness. I came back because I know what's happening. I know the family is falling apart, and I know I'm the one who caused it."

The other men shifted uncomfortably, their eyes flickering between me and Luka, waiting for his response.

Luka took another step closer, his eyes narrowing. "And what? You think you can just walk in here and fix everything? You think you can make up for the men who died because you weren't here?"

"I'm not here to make up for anything," I said quietly, my voice steady despite the storm of emotions inside me. "But I can't sit back and watch this family destroy itself. I made a mistake in leaving. A big one. And now I'm back to fix it, whether you want me here or not."

The tension in the room was thick, the air heavy with unspoken words. Luka stared at me for a long moment, his fists still clenched, his chest rising and falling with the force of his breath.

Finally, he spoke, his voice low and hard. "You think you're still our leader, Silas? You think you can just walk in here after abandoning us?"

"I don't know what I am anymore," I admitted, the weight of the truth pressing down on me like a heavy stone. "But I know one thing—I was wrong to leave. If you allow me, I will take the lead once more. But I won't pretend like everything is the same."

Luka's jaw tightened, his eyes flashing with a mixture of anger and pain. But he didn't move. He didn't speak. And that, for now, was enough.

The family was fractured, broken in ways I hadn't anticipated. But I could feel it in the way they looked at me—the hope, the desperation. They needed a leader, and for better or worse, I was still that man.

As much as I had tried to run from it, I couldn't escape the truth. The family was in my blood. It was a part of me, whether I liked it or not.

I couldn't run from my responsibilities any longer.

It was now my responsibility to gather the fragments.

Chapter 7

The morning light filtered through the warehouse windows, casting long shadows across the cold, concrete floor. The men—my men, now that I was back—stood silently around me, waiting for orders, waiting for a plan. Their faces were lined with exhaustion, tension hanging thick in the air. They had been struggling without me, being torn apart by rival families, greed, and chaos.

Luka stood at my side, his jaw tight and his eyes fixed on the ground, still bristling with resentment. He wasn't wrong to be angry; I had left them in the middle of a storm. But now that I was back, I needed him more than ever. I needed all of them.

I had been their leader once, and whether they knew it or not, they needed me to lead again.

I stepped forward, meeting their eyes, letting the silence settle over us like a shroud. The weight of everything I had abandoned was heavy in this room. The family had suffered a tremendous deal, and now was the moment to rescue it from its perilous state.

"We've been hit hard," I said, my voice steady. "But we aren't finished. Not yet."

The men shifted, their eyes flickering to mine. They were listening, but the trust wasn't fully there. Not yet. That would take time—time and action.

"We're going to rebuild," I continued, pacing slowly, feeling the energy shift as I spoke. "But this isn't about surviving anymore. It's about thriving. We don't simply rebuild and return to the previous state of affairs. No. We take back what's ours, and we make sure no one forgets what it means to cross us."

I could see the flicker of recognition in their eyes—the small spark of belief that had been buried under months of uncertainty. They were remembering who they were and who we were. The family wasn't just some group of thugs and criminals—it was a force. And it was time to remind the city of that fact.

"Business resumes today," I said, my voice hardening. "I want everyone back in position by the end of the week. Collections, protection—the whole operation. I don't care what it takes—bribes, threats, whatever you have to do. Make it happen."

Luka shifted beside me, his arms crossed over his broad chest. "And the families that hit us when you were gone?"

I paused, turning to face him. The question hung in the air between us, heavy and loaded with tension. This wasn't just about getting back on track—this was about revenge. I wanted to demonstrate to them that my absence didn't weaken the family. It wasn't to be crossed.

"They took advantage of us," I said, my voice dropping lower, colder. "And they'll pay for that. But we'll be smart about it. No reckless violence. We hit them where it hurts most."

I could see the men's faces harden, their jaws tightening as they thought about the families that had tried to take what was ours. The moment I left, they saw it as an opportunity—a chance to move in on our territory. They had underestimated us, and that was their first mistake.

"They thought we were vulnerable," I continued, my eyes scanning the room. "They thought we wouldn't fight back. They're wrong. And when we hit them, it won't just be about retaliation. It'll be about making sure no one ever tries this again."

I turned to Luka; my mind was already working through the details and logistics. I had to figure out who had hit us the hardest—who had been the first to strike. The city's underworld had always been a web of shifting alliances and quiet betrayals. But this time, it was personal.

"Start gathering intel," I said, my voice cold and calculating. I want to know who struck first, hardest, and had weaknesses. We're not just pursuing them; we're systematically dismantling them.

Luka gave me a curt nod, and I could see the fire in his eyes. He wanted this. They all did. But they needed direction; they needed me to tell them how to channel that rage and how to use it to rebuild what had been torn apart.

"I want a full report by tomorrow," I said, turning back to the rest of the men. "Get moving."

They dispersed quickly, their footsteps echoing through the warehouse as they moved to carry out my orders. The room emptied, leaving just Luka and me standing in the cold silence. He didn't speak at first; he just stared at me, his expression unreadable.

"You think it'll be that easy?" He finally asked, his voice low. "Are we just getting everything back up and running like nothing happened?"

I met his gaze, my jaw tightening. "No," I said. "But I don't care if it's easy. It needs to happen."

He grunted, crossing his arms over his chest again. "You've got a lot of men who aren't thrilled with you, Silas. They'll follow orders, sure, but they don't trust you."

I let out a breath, my hands curling into fists at my sides. "I'm not asking for their trust, not yet. I'm asking for their loyalty."

Luka shook his head, a bitter laugh escaping his lips. "Loyalty? Have you abandoned them to their fate? You're lucky they didn't turn on you the moment you walked through that door."

I took a step closer, my eyes narrowing. "They didn't turn on me because they know I'm the only one who can fix this. Whether they trust me or not doesn't matter. They need me."

Luka held my gaze for a long moment before finally nodding, his expression softening just a fraction. "Yeah," he muttered. "They do. But don't think that means they'll forgive you."

I didn't respond. I didn't need their forgiveness. I needed to rebuild and regain our dominance in the city. Everything else was secondary.

The rest of the day passed in a blur of meetings and plans, every minute spent laying the groundwork for the family's resurgence. I met with the heads of our operations, setting new expectations and making sure everyone knew what was at stake. No one questioned me directly, but I could feel their eyes on me, their doubt simmering just beneath the surface.

It would take time to earn back their full loyalty, but that wasn't my priority right now. Survival came first. Power followed.

By nightfall, I had everything in place. The businesses that had been abandoned were being reopened, our protection rackets re-established. The city had become a battleground in my absence, but I was determined to reclaim our territory, one block at a time.

As the last meeting ended and the men filed out of the warehouse, I finally had a moment to breathe. I leaned back in the worn chair, my eyes closing as I let the exhaustion wash over me.

However, the moment of peace was short-lived. My mind was still racing, still calculating the next move. There was no time for rest. Not yet.

Luka returned just after midnight, his expression grim. He dropped a folder onto the table in front of me, and I opened it without a word.

Inside were detailed reports on the families that had hit us during my absence. They provided the names, dates, and precise times of their attacks. Some were expected—old rivals, the ones who had always been looking for a way in. But one name stood out, one that I hadn't anticipated.

"The Echeverri family," Luka said, his voice low. "They made the first move. Took over three of our territories before anyone even knew what was happening."

I stared at the name; my blood was boiling as the realization sank in. The Echeverris were ruthless, but they had never been a threat to us before. They had always been small-time players, content to keep their heads down and their operations local.

Until now.

"They thought you weren't coming back," Luka continued, his jaw clenched. "Thought they could take over while we were vulnerable."

I clenched my fists, the rage bubbling up inside me. The Echeverris had always been insignificant, a nuisance at most. But now they had overstepped, and they were going to pay for it.

"They were wrong," I said, my voice cold and hard. "And now we're going to remind them why."

Luka nodded, a grim smile tugging at the corner of his mouth. "How do you want to play this?"

I closed the folder, my mind already working through the details. The Echeverris weren't just going to be dealt with—they were going to be annihilated. I wasn't interested in sending a message. I was interested in making sure no one ever dared cross us again.

"We hit them hard," I said, my voice steady. "And we don't stop until they're done."

Luka grinned, his eyes gleaming with anticipation. "That's what I wanted to hear."

The plan came together quickly, every detail meticulously calculated. The Echeverris wouldn't see it coming. We would target their most vulnerable areas, systematically dismantling their entire operation until it was reduced to nothing but ashes.

As I sat alone in the warehouse, the weight of what was to come settled over me. The family was coming back, but this time it would be different. This time, it wasn't just about power. It was about survival.

I had no intention of losing the game.

Chapter 8

The sun was barely up when I arrived at the warehouse, my mind racing with a mix of anticipation and dread. In the corner of the dimly lit space stood a figure I hadn't seen in years—a man who had always existed on the periphery of my life, part friend, part ghost. They called him "Ranger."

Ranger was never one for formality or the flashy bravado that so many in this life relied on. He was quiet, calculating, a man who moved in the shadows but commanded respect whenever he stepped into the light. When I was younger, still rising through the ranks, he was one of the few who never asked for anything and never wanted to be close to the power. Instead, he seemed content to observe from a distance, stepping in only when it was necessary.

However, now he was here. His unexpected appearance indicated that he was aware of my serious situation.

I walked toward him, my boots heavy on the concrete floor. Ranger looked up, his sharp eyes assessing me in a way that made me feel exposed, like he could see through everything I had built since my return. His face was as unreadable as ever.

"Silas," he said, nodding in acknowledgment. "You've made quite the mess for yourself."

I smirked at that. "Wouldn't be the first time."

Ranger crossed his arms over his chest, leaning back against the cold steel wall. He wasn't the kind of man to jump straight into a conversation. He preferred to feel things out first, to let the silence do its work.

I could tell he was here for a reason, and I wasn't in the mood for games. "Why are you here, Ranger?"

He raised an eyebrow, his lips twitching into what appeared to be a faint smile. "You're back, and things are moving again. However, you and I both understand that the city has undergone significant changes. You can't run things the way you used to. Not after everything."

I shifted my weight, feeling the truth of his words settle in. "And you think you can help me with that?"

Ranger nodded, his gaze never leaving mine. "Not think. Know."

There was a pause, and then I stepped closer, leaning in slightly, my voice low. "You're not the type to get involved in something unless there's something in it for you. So, what do you want?"

Ranger's eyes darkened, and for the first time, there was a flash of something behind his calm exterior. "What I want is for the city to stop tearing itself apart. You think the Echeverris are the only ones who've been taking shots at your family? No. It's worse than you know."

I frowned. I had been focused on the Echeverris, but Ranger hinted at something more dangerous.

"Who else?" I asked, my jaw tightening.

"The moment you disappeared, the sharks started circling," Ranger said, pushing off the wall and stepping toward me. "It's not just the Echeverris. Other clans have been moving in, testing the waters, seeing how much they can take before someone steps up."

He paused, giving me a stern look. "And no one's been stepping up."

His words cut deep, not because they weren't true, but because they confirmed the nagging feeling that had been gnawing at me since my return. The family was weakened and vulnerable, and if I didn't act fast, we'd be wiped out.

"So what do you suggest?" I posed the question, crossing my arms over my chest. "You know how this works. We can't just go in guns blazing."

Ranger nodded, his expression serious. "No, we can't. However, we cannot passively wait for them to approach us. You need to show strength. You need to remind everyone who you are and what the family stands for."

I felt the weight of his words, but there was something more in the way he said it, like he had already been working on a plan.

"And I assume you have a way to do that?" I asked.

Ranger reached into his jacket, pulling out a folded piece of paper. He handed it to me without a word, and I unfolded it, my eyes scanning the list of names and locations. These were targets—members of rival clans, businesses that had been seized in my absence.

"This is where we start," Ranger said, his voice low and calm. "You hit these places hard, but smart. Show them that you're back and that you're not afraid to take control again. And when the smoke clears, they'll think twice before coming after your family again."

I stared at the list; the cold realization settled over me. Ranger wasn't just talking about retaliation—this was a calculated strike, a way to send a message to everyone in the city that the family wasn't dead yet.

I folded the paper and slipped it into my jacket. "What's your role in all of this?"

Ranger shrugged, his face unreadable again. "I help where I can. You're going to need someone who can move in the shadows, someone who knows how to get things done without attracting attention. I can be that person."

There was no hesitation in his voice, no doubt. He wasn't offering to follow me blindly, but there was a trust between us, an understanding that we both needed this to work. I didn't have many people I could rely on in this world, but Ranger had always been someone who saw things clearly, who never got caught up in the power games that consumed so many others.

I nodded, feeling a sense of purpose settle over me. "Alright. Let's get to work."

The next few days passed in a blur of planning and action. Ranger and I worked side by side, mapping out each move with surgical precision. We gathered intel on the rival clans, learned where they were weakest, and identified the key players who had been orchestrating the attacks against my family.

The first strike was set for Thursday night.

It was a modest operation, lacking in grandeur but sufficient to convey a message. One of the rival clan's businesses had been taken over recently, a warehouse they were using to store shipments coming in from the docks. It was the perfect place to remind them who was in control.

Ranger and I stood on the roof of an abandoned building across the street, watching as the men moved in and out of the warehouse below. The silence was eerie, akin to that which precedes a storm. The air was thick with tension, and I could feel the adrenaline building in my veins.

"Ready?" Ranger asked, his voice low.

I nodded, my eyes never leaving the warehouse. "Let's do this."

The plan was simple. A small team of my most trusted men would move in, take out the guards, and seize the shipment. There would be no needless violence, just a clean operation to reassure them that we would not be intimidated.

As the men moved in, I felt a strange sense of calm wash over me. This was what I was excelling at—this was where I thrived. The stress, the risks, and the understanding that each choice was significant were all present. It was a stark contrast to the life I had tried to build in the shadows, away from all of this.

However, as much as I hated to admit it, this was where I belonged.

The operation proceeded smoothly. The guards were taken down quickly, and the shipment was secured. By the time we left, the rival clan would know exactly who was behind it, and they'd think twice before coming after us again.

Ranger and I stood on the rooftop, watching as the men finished up below. He turned to me, his expression unreadable.

"Good work," he said, his voice calm. "This is just the beginning, though. You know that, right?"

I nodded, my jaw tight. "Yeah. I know."

There was a long pause before Ranger spoke again. "You're not the same as you were before, Silas. I can see it. But if you're going to lead again, if you're going to rebuild this family, you need to figure out who you are now."

His words hung in the air, heavy and sharp. I wanted to argue, to tell him that I was still the same man I had always been. But deep down, I knew he was right. Something had changed in me. The time I spent away, trying to run from my past, had left its mark.

Still, as I stood there, watching the warehouse below, I realised something else. I could never truly escape this life. The family, the power, the control—it was all part of who I was, whether I liked it or not.

I turned to Ranger, my eyes hard. "I know who I am," I said, my voice steady. "And I know what needs to be done."

Ranger nodded, his eyes glinting with something that might've been approval. "Good. Because we've got a lot of work ahead of us."

The attacks continued over the next few weeks, each one more calculated and precise than the last. The rival clans were scrambling, trying to hold on to the territory they had taken, but it was too late. With Ranger's help, I was dismantling them piece by piece.

And as the family regained its power, I could feel the old fire burning inside me again. The doubt, the fear—it was all falling away, replaced by a single, burning purpose.

I wasn't running anymore.

I was taking back what was mine.

Chapter 9

The wind whispered through the cracked windows of the old estate, and every creak of the floorboards beneath my boots felt heavier than it should. The walls of this house—once a symbol of strength and power—now seemed like a prison. I had returned to claim what was rightfully mine, but what had I really come back to? A fractured family, a kingdom in shambles. Every corner felt like it held a secret, and every shadow seemed ready to betray me.

Ranger's words still echoed in my mind, gnawing at my gut like an infection I couldn't cure. **Not everyone is loyal,** he'd said with that quiet intensity that meant he was certain of it. And Ranger was never wrong. He had been my closest confidant, the one man I could rely on when things fell apart. But hearing that some within my own family—the men I had bled with and grown up with—could be plotting against me was like swallowing glass.

I couldn't show my weakness. The pressure was intensifying from all directions. I pushed open the heavy door to the meeting room, where half a dozen of my men sat around a long table, their eyes snapping to me as soon as I entered. Some of them had been with me since the beginning, but who could I trust now?

I took my seat at the head of the table, feeling the weight of their gazes pressing on me. Every flicker of movement, every cough, or shift in posture set my nerves on edge. Were they watching me with loyalty, or were they waiting for me to stumble?

"We've had some losses," I began, my voice steady despite the turmoil inside me. "But this is only the beginning of our resurgence. We're not dead yet."

The words felt hollow even as I spoke them. Ranger sat to my right, his expression unreadable, but I knew he was scanning the room just as I was—looking for any hint of betrayal. The others nodded, some of them murmuring in agreement, but I could sense the unease beneath their stoic faces. They had followed me back here because they thought I could lead them to victory, to power, and to the top of the criminal world once again. But was I that leader? Or was I just a man with blood on his hands, trying to outrun a past that would never let go?

The betrayal wasn't just a whisper anymore. It was a reality that loomed over me like a dark cloud, and I didn't know who the traitor was. Was it Rocco, the one who always kept to himself but had been fiercely loyal to Carlo before me? Could it be Dom, the outspoken individual with significant stakes in the outcome? My mind raced with possibilities, paranoia tightening its grip around my throat.

The meeting ended, but the tension didn't leave the room with the men. Ranger stayed behind, his sharp eyes studying me as he leaned against the edge of the table.

"You still think you can trust all of them?" He asked quietly, his voice barely above a whisper, but there was no need to speak louder. The walls in this house had ears.

I didn't answer right away. Instead, I looked out the window at the estate grounds. Once, I felt proud to call this place mine. Now, I wasn't so sure.

"Not everyone," I said finally. "But I need them, Ranger. I can't run this alone."

"Sure, I need them," Ranger said, pushing off the table and taking a step closer. "But don't be blind. Whoever's pulling the strings behind your back, they're waiting for the right moment. And when they strike, it won't just be you who pays the price."

His words hit harder than I wanted to admit. I ran a hand through my hair, feeling the familiar burn of frustration rise in my chest. I hated being out of control. I hated not knowing who to trust. But more than that, I hated the thought of failure.

"I'll find out who it is," I muttered, more to myself than to Ranger. "And when I do, they'll wish they never crossed me."

Ranger nodded, but his eyes showed doubt that gave me a queasy stomach. "You better do it fast, Silas. Things are already unravelling."

The unravelling came faster than I expected.

It started with a phone call, just as the sun began to set, casting long shadows over the estate. A family-owned bar, one of our quieter, low-key businesses, had been hit. Not just hit, but **massacred**. My heart pounded as I listened to the voice on the other end of the line describe the scene. Broken glass, bodies, blood—so much blood. I gripped the phone tight enough that my knuckles turned white.

"How many dead?" I asked, my voice rough.

The answer was "six," and it felt like a punch to the gut. "Three of them were ours. The rest... civilians."

Civilians. The war had spiraled out of control, trapping innocent lives in its crossfire. I wanted to punch something, to scream, to tear apart the walls of this cursed house and let all the buried secrets come pouring out. Instead, I clenched my teeth and compelled myself to maintain my composure.

"Who did this?" I demanded.

"Looks like one of the rival families—Vincenti's crew. But there's no solid proof."

Vincenti. Since Carlo's passing, that individual had been circling us like a vulture, anticipating the opportunity to dismember us. And now he had made his move. I hung up the phone and stared at the floor, my mind spinning. This wasn't just an attack on our business. This was personal. This was a message.

And the message was clear: I wasn't in control anymore.

The hours that followed were a blur of frantic decisions, meetings, and plans. My men were on edge, more nervous than I had ever seen them. The attack had rattled them, and I could see the doubt in their eyes. They didn't say it out loud, but I could feel it in the air—**they were starting to doubt me.**

Was I losing my grip? Was I becoming weak, just like Carlo in his final days?

I wanted to lash out, to scream at them that I was still their leader, that I was still strong. But deep down, I knew the truth. The cracks were starting to show, and no matter how hard I tried to hold everything together, the foundation was crumbling beneath me.

I stood in the bathroom later that night, staring at my reflection in the mirror. The man looking back at me wasn't the man I used to be. There were bags under my eyes, the skin drawn tight from sleepless nights. My jaw was clenched, and the muscles tightened from too much tension and anger. And my eyes... they were hard, cold. I barely recognised myself.

I splashed cold water on my face, trying to shake the feeling of failure that clung to me like a shadow. I had come back to take control, to lead the family out of the chaos that Carlo had left behind. But now, all I could see was the blood. The bodies. The destruction.

Was it my fault? Had I failed them? **Had I failed myself?**

I turned off the faucet and braced my hands against the sink, my head hanging low. Ranger's words echoed in my mind. **They'll wish they never crossed me.**

However, what if I wasn't enough? What if I wasn't strong enough to pull us out of this mess?

I felt a surge of anger rise in my chest—anger at Vincenti, anger at the traitor in my midst, but most of all, anger at myself. I was supposed to be better than this. I was supposed to be **in control**.

And yet here I was, on the verge of losing everything.

The next day, I gathered my men. We stood in the old warehouse, the air thick with tension. Some of them avoided my gaze; others watched me with wary eyes. Ranger stood by my side, his presence a quiet reminder that I wasn't alone in this. But even with him there, I felt the weight of doubt pressing down on me.

"Vincenti thinks he can hit us and get away with it," I said, my voice steady but cold. "He's wrong."

The men nodded, but there was no fire in their eyes. They were tired, just like I was. Tired of the constant fighting, the bloodshed, the uncertainty. I had to give them something—**something to believe in again.**

"We're going to hit back," I continued. "Hard. We're going to make sure that every family in this city knows what happens when you cross us."

There was a murmur of agreement, but it was half-hearted. I could see the doubt still lingering in the corners of their minds. They were waiting for something more, something that would reignite the fire that had once driven us.

"We lost people last night," I said, my voice quieter now. "Good people. People who trusted us to protect them. And we failed them."

Silence fell over the room. I could see the guilt in their eyes—the same guilt that gnawed at me.

"But we can't afford to fall apart," I said, my voice growing stronger. "Not now. Not when the wolves are circling."

I looked around the room, meeting each of their gazes. "I need you with me. All of you. Because if we fall now, if we let this slip through our fingers, it's over. Everything Carlo built, everything we fought for—it's gone."

They were listening now, really listening. I could see the flicker of determination returning, slowly but surely. I had to believe in myself, even if it was the hardest thing to do right now. If I didn't, everything would collapse.

"We're going to make Vincenti pay," I said, my voice like steel. "And we're going to find out who's been stabbing us in the back. Because I'm not losing this family. Not again."

The room was silent for a moment, and then Ranger spoke up, his voice low but firm. "We're with you, Silas."

One by one, the others nodded. It wasn't much, but it was enough for now.

As I left the warehouse, the weight of leadership pressed harder on my shoulders. The betrayal still lingered in the air, and I knew the attack wasn't the last. But for now, I had my men. And I had to believe that was enough.

For now.

Chapter 10

The old study was one of the few rooms in the estate that still held some of its former grandeur. The dark wood panelling, the heavy velvet curtains, and the towering bookshelves lined with volumes that hadn't been touched in years created a sense of permanence, as if time itself couldn't erode the secrets held within these walls. I stood in the center of the room. The dim light from the desk lamp cast long shadows over the floor. The scent of aged leather and dust filled my lungs as I stared at the scattered papers in front of me.

These papers were more than old business records—they were pieces of my family's history, pieces that had been hidden from me for years. I discovered a ledger filled with peculiar notations, several yellowed letters penned by my father, and a sealed envelope bearing my name. I had found them buried deep in Carlo's personal vault, tucked away as if they were meant to stay hidden forever.

The ledger was the first thing that caught my attention. At first glance, it appeared to be a simple financial record, but something about it didn't sit right with me. The dates and amounts didn't add up to any of the businesses I knew about, and the names scribbled in the margins were unfamiliar. I flipped through the pages, my heart pounding with a growing sense of unease. Carlo had always prided himself on being transparent with me when it came to family business, but this was something different. Something darker.

I slammed the book shut, my hands shaking with a mixture of anger and fear. What had my father been hiding? What was this?

I grabbed the envelope with my name on it and tore it open. The paper inside was fragile, its edges crumbling slightly as I unfolded it. The handwriting was unmistakable—Carlo's—but the words that followed made my blood run cold.

Silas,

If you're reading this, it means you've found what I had hoped you never would. By now, you've likely begun to see the cracks in the story I told you, the one about our rise to power. You've always been strong, but strength doesn't come without a price.

There are things about our family—about me—that I never wanted you to know. I did what I had to do, not for myself but for you. For the family. But the truth is, our empire was built on a foundation of lies.

You need to understand, Silas, that everything I did was meant to protect us.

The letter fell from my hands, landing silently on the desk. I stumbled back, my legs barely holding me up as the weight of the words crushed down on me. Lies. Everything I had been raised to believe—the code of honor, the pride in our family's power, and the legacy that I had killed to protect—was all built on deception. My father, who I had idolized for so long, wasn't the man I thought he was.

What had he done? What was the truth he was desperately trying to conceal?

I staggered back to the desk, my eyes burning as I forced myself to read the rest of the letter.

There are things I've done, Silas, that I'm not proud of. I've made deals and trusted people that I shouldn't have. I had intended it for the family's future, but it became about survival.

When you discover what I did, you'll hate me. But I need you to know that everything I did was for you. You were my only hope, Silas. You still are.

I'm sorry.

I sank into the chair behind the desk, my head spinning. Everything I had fought for, everything I had sacrificed—it was all a lie. I wanted to scream, to tear apart the room, to burn every last remnant of the life I had been forced to live. But instead, I just sat there, numb.

How could Carlo do this to me? How could he lie to me, to his own son, while making me believe I was following in his righteous footsteps? I had killed for this family, buried my conscience in the dirt alongside the bodies of my enemies. And for what? A legacy of betrayal?

The door creaked open behind me, but I didn't turn around. I didn't need to. I knew it was Ranger.

"You've been in here a while," he said quietly, his voice breaking the heavy silence. "Find something interesting?"

I didn't answer at first. My throat felt dry, and my mind was still reeling from the revelation. I stared at the papers on the desk, feeling the weight of Carlo's betrayal pressing down on me.

"I found the truth," I said finally, my voice barely above a whisper.

Ranger stepped closer, his presence steady and calming, but I couldn't bring myself to look at him. I didn't want him to see the cracks in my armor—the vulnerability that I had worked so hard to bury.

"What truth?" he asked, his tone cautious.

I handed him the letter without a word. I heard the rustle of paper as he unfolded it, and then the silence as he read. When he finished, he let out a low breath.

"So… Carlo wasn't who you thought he was," Ranger said softly, more of a statement than a question.

I shook my head, feeling a bitter laugh rise in my throat. "No. He wasn't."

Ranger was silent for a long moment, and when he finally spoke, his voice was thoughtful. "You always said Carlo was a complicated man. Maybe this was part of that."

"Complicated?" I snapped, the anger bubbling up before I could stop it. "He was a liar, Ranger. Everything he built, everything I've been fighting for—it's all based on lies."

"And now you're questioning why you came back," Ranger said quietly, reading me as easily as if I were an open book.

I clenched my fists, my nails digging into my palms. He was right. The question had been gnawing at me ever since I found that letter. **Was it worth it? Was anything I was doing worth it?**

"I don't know who I am anymore," I admitted, my voice cracking under the weight of the confession. "I thought I was fighting for something real. But now… now I don't know."

Ranger pulled up a chair and sat across from me, his eyes locked on mine. "Listen, Silas. I've been with you a long time. I've seen what you're capable of and what you've sacrificed. And I'm telling you, you're more than just Carlo's son. You're more than the lies he built."

I looked away, unable to meet his gaze. The truth was, I didn't feel like anything more. I felt like a shadow, a hollow shell of the man I used to be. And the worst part? I didn't even know if I wanted to keep fighting.

Ranger reached across the desk, tapping his fingers on the scattered papers. "This doesn't define you," he said firmly. "Carlo's mistakes aren't your mistakes."

"But they are," I argued, my voice rising. "Don't you get it? Everything I've done, everything I've become—it's because of him. I followed his path, his rules. And now... now I'm stuck in this nightmare, trying to keep a family together that might not even be worth saving."

Ranger leaned back in his chair, studying me with a quiet intensity. "Is that what you really think? That it's not worth saving?"

I hesitated, the answer hanging in the air like a weight on my chest. Was the family worth saving? Was this life, this endless cycle of violence and betrayal, worth the cost?

"I don't know," I whispered, the words tasting bitter on my tongue. "I don't know anymore."

Ranger was silent for a moment, and then he stood, his expression unreadable. "You know, Silas, the family isn't just about the power. It's about the people. The men who look to you, who trust you to lead them. You think they care about Carlo's lies? No. They care about you. You're their leader. Their hope."

Hope. The word felt foreign to me. I hadn't felt hope in a long time. But Ranger's words stirred something deep inside me, something I had buried long ago. The weight of leadership, the responsibility to those who followed me—it was crushing, yes. But it was also what gave me purpose. What kept me from drowning in the darkness.

"I'm not the man they think I am," I said, my voice rough.

"No one ever is," Ranger replied. "But that doesn't mean you're not the leader they need."

I looked at him then, really looked at him, and for the first time in a long while, I felt a flicker of something other than despair. Ranger had always been my rock, the one person who had my back no matter what. And now, as I faced the darkest truth of my life, he was still here, still standing beside me.

But even as that flicker of hope began to take root, something in Ranger's eyes made my stomach twist. There was a heaviness there—a weight that hadn't been there before.

"There's something else, isn't there?" I asked, my voice low.

Ranger didn't answer right away. He crossed his arms over his chest, his jaw tight. I could see the struggle in his eyes, the hesitation.

"I didn't want to tell you," he said finally, his voice barely above a whisper. "But I can't keep it from you anymore."

A cold dread washed over me, my heart pounding in my chest. "Tell me what?"

Ranger took a deep breath, his eyes locking onto mine. "The girl you saved. The one with the broken foot. She wasn't just some random woman. She was working for Vincenti."

The room seemed to tilt, the walls closing in on me as Ranger's words sank in. **The girl. The one I had risked everything to save. She had betrayed me.**

"She was sent to find you," Ranger continued, his voice heavy with regret. "To lure you out."

My mind reeled, the betrayal hitting me like a physical blow. I had helped her and protected her. And all along, she had been working against me.

"How do you know?" I demanded, my voice shaking with fury.

"We intercepted a message," Ranger said quietly. "She gave them your location."

The rage that surged through me was like nothing I had ever felt before. I had been a fool. A blind, trusting fool. And now, because of that, everything was at risk.

"I should have let her die," I muttered, my fists clenching.

Ranger shook his head. "That's not who you are, Silas."

"Maybe it should be," I spat, the words bitter and sharp.

However, deep down, I knew he was right. As much as I hated to admit it, letting her die wasn't the answer. It wasn't who I was. Not yet, at least.

But the betrayal cut deep. And now, more than ever, I was beginning to wonder if I could survive in a world where trust was a luxury I could no longer afford.

And worse, I was beginning to wonder if I even wanted to try.

The weight of everything was unbearable, and as I stared at the scattered papers on the desk, the fractured pieces of my past, I realised something. **This wasn't just about power. It wasn't about vengeance. It was about survival—my survival.**

And in this world, there was no room for weakness.

Chapter 11

The smell of gunpowder and blood hung heavy in the air as I stood in the centre of the wreckage. My men were spread out around me, checking the bodies and clearing the area. It had been a brutal fight—the kind that leaves you with that gnawing emptiness deep in your gut. Another rival clan had dared to strike, and once again, I'd had to retaliate harder than before, each move pushing me further away from the man I thought I could be. Every time I stepped into the violence, I found myself slipping a little further from the dream of escape.

The cracked asphalt beneath my boots was still slick with rain, now tinged red with the blood of those foolish enough to cross us. I should've felt some sense of victory, some sick satisfaction in knowing we'd won, but all I felt was exhaustion. The weight of my family's legacy was dragging me down, and with every punch I threw and every shot I fired, I could feel myself sinking deeper into the darkness.

"Clear," Ranger's voice called out from behind me.

I turned to see him wiping his knife clean, his eyes scanning the area with that same calm, calculated look he always had. His presence was the only thing I trusted, but it felt like the walls were closing in.

"Any word on the others?" I asked, knowing full well the answer.

"They took some heavy losses," he said, sheathing the knife. "But nothing that'll stop them from hitting back. If anything, this is only going to make them angrier."

I clenched my fists, my blood boiling. These clans—they were like vultures, circling, waiting for a sign of weakness. And ever since I came back, they'd been testing me, pushing the limits. This wasn't just about control anymore; it was about survival. And the only way to survive in this world was to show no mercy.

However, with every decision I made and every order I gave, I could feel something slipping inside me. I wasn't the same man I was when I first walked away. And I didn't know if I could ever go back.

Ranger walked up beside me, looking at the scene with the same detachment that always unnerved me. He had seen it all before and had lived this life for as long as I had. However, he didn't seem to experience the same level of shock as I did.

"They'll come at us again, you know," he said, lighting a cigarette. "Sooner or later."

"They won't get the chance," I muttered, my jaw tightening. "Next time, I'm ending it."

Ranger took a drag from his cigarette and exhaled slowly, his eyes narrowing as he glanced at me. "You're playing a dangerous game, Silas. You go after them like that, and there's no coming back."

I looked away, feeling the weight of his words settle in. Maybe that was the point. Maybe I didn't want to come back. The man I was before could not survive in this world. I wasn't sure I even wanted to survive in this world.

Before I could respond, a shout came from one of my men near the edge of the lot.

"Boss! We've got someone!"

I turned, my hand instinctively going to the gun at my hip as I made my way toward the voice. A man was on the ground, bloodied and barely conscious, but alive enough to speak. He was a member of the rival clan, having led the charge against us.

I crouched down, grabbing him by the collar and pulling him up so that he had no choice but to look me in the eye. "Who sent you?"

The man groaned, his face twisted in pain, but he didn't answer. His defiance only fuelled the fire burning in my chest.

"Who sent you?" I repeated, my voice low and dangerous.

His eyes flickered with fear, but he still didn't speak.

I could feel my patience wearing thin, the darkness inside me growing. Without thinking, I drew my gun and pressed it against his temple. "Last chance."

"Silas—" Ranger's voice was cautious, but I ignored him.

The man's lips trembled, but he finally muttered something under his breath. I leaned in closer.

"Vincenti," he croaked. "It was Vincent."

Vincenti. The name felt like a knife twisting in my gut. Of course it was him. He had been patiently waiting for the ideal opportunity to act. And now, with Carlo gone and me back in the fold, he was coming for blood.

I released the man, letting him slump back onto the ground and stand up. My mind was racing, the adrenaline surging through my veins.

Vincenti. It had always been him. And now he was about to feel the full force of everything I'd been holding back.

The drive back to the estate was intense. The rain had picked up again, the windscreen wipers struggling to keep up as the storm raged outside. Ranger sat in the passenger seat, his eyes forward, not saying much, but I could feel his unease.

"You're thinking about going after him, aren't you?" he finally asked, breaking the silence.

"I'm not thinking about it," I said, my knuckles white as I gripped the steering wheel. "I'm doing it."

Ranger sighed, running a hand through his hair. "Look, I get it. Vincenti's a snake. But you go after him like this, and it's not just him you're taking down. You're dragging the whole family into a war."

"It's already a war," I shot back. "He escalated it. I'm just finishing it."

"And what's the cost, Silas?" Ranger's voice was firm, but there was an edge of concern. "How far are you willing to go before you lose yourself completely?"

I didn't answer. Because the truth was, I didn't know.

As we arrived at the estate, Carlo's lies, the ongoing threat from rival clans, and the responsibility of leading a family in disarray all weighed heavily on me. And then there was the guilt. I felt the remorse for selecting this life, understanding that each choice I made distanced me from the tranquil future Lena and I had once envisioned.

I killed that future the moment I pulled the trigger on Carlo.

Back inside the estate, I tried to focus on the task at hand. I needed to plan to gather the men and make the necessary moves to eliminate Vincenti before he could strike again. But no matter how hard I tried, I couldn't shake the growing unease gnawing at me.

And then she appeared.

It was late, and most of the men had already retired for the night, but I heard the sound of the front door opening and closing softly. I turned from the window, my heart freezing in my chest as I saw her standing in the doorway.

It was her. The woman from the rocks. The one I had saved.

She looked different now—more put together, more confident. But there was something else in her eyes, something that set off alarm bells in my head. She wasn't here by accident. She wasn't here because she was lost or broken.

She was here with a purpose.

"What are you doing here?" I demanded, my voice cold.

She didn't flinch. She stepped further into the room, her eyes locked on mine. "We need to talk."

"We have nothing to talk about," I snapped, but she didn't back down.

"You saved my life," she said, her voice steady. "And I didn't repay that debt. But now, I'm here to give you something in return."

"I don't want anything from you."

"You don't have a choice," she said, stepping closer. "You think you can fight this war on your own? You can't. Not without my help."

I stared at her, my pulse quickening. "What are you talking about?"

"I know Vincenti," she said, her eyes narrowing. "I know how he operates. And I know what he's planning."

The room felt like it was closing in around me, the tension thick enough to choke on. She wasn't just some random woman caught in the crossfire—she was a part of this. She always had been.

"What's your angle?" I asked, my voice low and dangerous.

She smiled, but there was no warmth in it. "My angle is survival, Silas. Same as yours."

I didn't trust her. Hell, I didn't trust anyone anymore. But as much as I wanted to throw her out, I knew deep down that she had information I needed.

"Tell me what you know," I said, crossing my arms over my chest.

She hesitated for a moment, then stepped even closer, her voice dropping to a whisper. "Vincenti's planning something big. Something that will wipe out your family for good."

My jaw clenched, the anger boiling just beneath the surface. "What is it?"

"I'll tell you," she said, her eyes locking onto mine. "But I want something in return."

"Of course you do," I muttered, already tired of this game. "What do you want?"

She stepped closer, her voice barely a whisper now. "I want out. I want to disappear, just like you tried to. I've been trapped in this life for too long, and I can't do it anymore."

I stared at her, my mind racing. She was offering me the key to taking down Vincenti, but in return, she wanted to vanish. Could I trust her? Was she really willing to betray him, or was this just another one of Vincenti's traps?

"Why should I believe you?" I asked, my voice cold.

"Because," she said, her eyes dark with intensity, "I'm the only one who can get you close enough to kill him."

The room was suffocating, the weight of her offer hanging in the air between us. I felt the walls closing in on me, the choices narrowing until there was no good option left.

She represented everything I had tried to leave behind—the manipulation, the deceit, the violence. But no matter how far I ran, it always found me again. **Now, here I was, faced with a choice that would determine everything.**

Trust her and use her to take down Vincenti, or turn her away and risk losing everything. Either way, I was walking deeper into the darkness.

And no matter what I chose, I knew I'd never be the same.

As I stared into her eyes, I realised something—**this was the life I was born into.** The violence, the betrayal, the bloodshed—it was all part of the legacy I carried. I could never escape it, no matter how hard I tried.

Still, now, more than ever, I had to decide. Was I willing to sacrifice the last shred of humanity I had left? Or was there still a way out? **The choice lay before me**—to end the threat of Vincenti and lose myself completely, or let her walk away and risk everything I had fought for.

And as the silence stretched on, I knew this moment would define me.

The choice was mine. But no matter what I decided, one thing was certain.

There was no turning back.

Chapter 12

The plan had been set for weeks. We meticulously planned each step and strategically placed each man. I had mapped out the attack against one of our biggest rivals, the Ferranti clan, with surgical precision. It was supposed to be a clean, decisive blow. We'd hit them hard enough that they wouldn't be able to retaliate. It was the kind of statement that would send ripples through every family in the underworld: *Silas is back, and he's not here to play.*

However, nothing ever goes as planned.

I stood at the edge of the industrial district, looking out over the flickering lights of warehouses and factories where the Ferrantis operated. This was their heart, their supply line for everything—from weapons to smuggling routes. If we took it, they'd be crippled, unable to recover.

Next to me, Ranger was silent, his presence a steadying force. He'd been with me through every battle, through every loss and win.

Now, he was more than just an advisor; he was my anchor, the one person I trusted in a world that was collapsing around me.

With a low voice and his eyes scanning the horizon, Ranger asked, "You ready?"

I nodded, feeling the familiar rush of adrenaline spike through my veins. The battle ahead didn't frighten me; it was the uncertain future that awaited. *You never know who you'll become after getting into a war.*

"The teams are in position," I said, maintaining a calm voice despite the internal turmoil I was experiencing. "It's time."

Ranger gave me a brief nod before adjusting his coat and checking his weapon. "Let's end this."

The assault began like clockwork. Our men moved in from every angle, guns drawn, moving silently in the shadows of the warehouses. The Ferrantis had no idea what was coming.

Within minutes, gunfire erupted, a sharp contrast to the quiet night. The warehouses were lit up by muzzle flashes, followed by the sound of men shouting, glass shattering, and the heavy thud of bodies hitting the ground.

I kept my focus sharp, taking out anyone in my path with ruthless efficiency. This wasn't personal. It was business. That's what I kept telling myself as the blood sprayed and the bodies fell. But deep down, I knew that wasn't true anymore.

Everything becomes personal when you have everything at stake.

Ranger was at my side, moving just as swiftly and coldly. We cut through the Ferrantis like a blade of cloth, making our way deeper into their hearts. It felt too easy—almost too smooth. That's when the dread set in, a gnawing feeling that something was about to go terribly wrong.

And then it did.

An explosion ripped through the warehouse behind us, the shockwave sending debris and fire into the air. I turned, horror spreading through my chest as I saw our men scattered, some already down, others scrambling for cover. The Ferrantis had set a trap. They knew we were coming.

"Ranger!" I shouted, but the chaos swallowed my voice.

I couldn't find him in the smoke and fire. The world around me blurred as I sprinted through the wreckage, dodging bullets and explosions, searching for the one person I couldn't afford to lose.

Another explosion shook the ground, and that's when I saw him—Ranger, lying on the ground, blood pooling beneath him.

"No," I whispered, running to him. "No, no, no."

He was still breathing, but barely. Shrapnel had torn through his side; his eyes glazed over with pain. I dropped to my knees beside him, my hands shaking as I pressed down on the wound, trying to stop the bleeding.

"Silas…" His voice was weak, barely a whisper.

"Don't talk," I said, panic clawing at my throat. "You're going to be fine. I'll get you out of here."

However, even as I said the words, I knew they were a lie. The blood wasn't stopping. It was pouring out faster than I could contain it. I could feel his life slipping away right in front of me, and there was nothing I could do.

"Silas… listen…" Ranger gasped, his hand gripping mine weakly. "You... you have to finish this."

"I'm not leaving you," I growled, my chest tightening with fear.

He shook his head, his breath coming in shallowly. "You have to. This isn't... over yet."

I felt the tears sting my eyes, but I pushed them down. I couldn't break. Not now. Not when everything was falling apart. But looking at him—my friend, my brother in all but blood—it felt like the world was crumbling around me.

"You've always been there, Ranger," I whispered, my voice cracking. "You can't leave me now."

His eyes softened, and for a moment, the pain seemed to fade. "You don't need me... Silas. You never did."

I shook my head, the denial clawing at my throat. "That's not true. I'm nothing without you."

He managed a weak smile, his hand tightening around mine. "You're stronger than you think. You... you're the leader they need."

Before I could respond, another explosion went off nearby, shaking the ground beneath us. I looked up, heart pounding, as the rest of the Ferrantis started to regroup. The fight wasn't over.

"Go," Ranger rasped. "Go, Silas."

My vision blurred as I stared at him, torn between saving him and finishing what we started. But his grip on my hand loosened, his eyes closing as his strength faded. He was telling me to let go. He was telling me to finish this.

How could I? How could I leave him here, bleeding out, when I owed him everything?

"I'll be back," I promised, my voice hoarse. "I swear it."

With a heavy heart, I stood up, drawing my weapon again as the rage bubbled up inside me. The Ferrantis had taken enough from me. They had taken everything.

They were about to make the payment.

The battle was a blur after that. All I could see was red—blood and fire and bodies hitting the ground. I fought with a fury I hadn't felt in years, my vision narrowing as I cut down anyone who stood in my way.

I was lost in it—the violence, the chaos. The need for revenge drowned out every other thought in my mind. All I wanted was to make them pay. I wanted them to endure the consequences of their actions towards Ranger.

By the time the last of the Ferrantis fell, the warehouse was nothing but a smoldering ruin. The air was thick with smoke, and the ground was littered with bodies—both theirs and ours. But I didn't feel any satisfaction. There was no victory here. Only loss.

I stumbled back to where Ranger had fallen, my heart in my throat. But when I reached the spot, he was gone.

"No…" I whispered, my chest tightening with panic.

I searched frantically, my mind racing. He couldn't be gone. He couldn't—

Then I saw him, leaning against a crate, barely conscious but alive.

"Ranger!" I rushed to him, my hands shaking as I crouched down beside him. "You're still here."

He gave me a weak smile, his face pale. "Told you… I'm not that simple to kill."

I let out a shaky breath, relief flooding through me. But the fear still gnawed at the edges of my mind. He wasn't out of the woods yet. He was still bleeding, still weak.

"We need to get you out of here," I said, my voice urgent. "You need a doctor."

Ranger nodded weakly, but I could see the pain in his eyes. He wasn't going to make it far like this.

"Stay with me," I whispered, my throat tightening. "Don't you dare die on me."

However, as I lifted him, the reality of the situation sank in. He was slipping. Fast.

Hours later, back at the estate, the doctor worked on Ranger in one of the back rooms while I paced the halls like a caged animal.

My hands were still stained with blood—his blood, their blood— and no matter how many times I washed them, it wouldn't come off.

I had lost control. In my need for revenge, I had let the violence consume me. And now Ranger was paying the price.

The door to the back room creaked open, and the doctor stepped out, wiping his hands on a cloth.

"He's stable, for now," the doctor said, his face grim. "But he's lost a lot of blood. If he makes it through the night, he'll have a chance."

I nodded, my throat too tight to speak. I had brought him back. But for how long?

As I stood there, staring at the door, the weight of everything crashed down on me. This wasn't what I had wanted. This wasn't the life I had dreamed of. I had come back to protect my family and to stop the chaos. But all I had done was cause more pain, more death.

And now, I was starting to wonder if I was even capable of saving them. Perhaps I was simply pulling them down with me.

I walked outside, the cool night air hitting my face as I tried to clear my head. The stars were bright overhead, the world silent except for the distant hum of the city.

For the first time since I came back, I felt truly alone.

The violence, the bloodshed—it was all consuming me. And in trying to lead, I was losing myself, piece by piece. I had thought I could fix this. I had thought I could save my family.

Still, now, standing under the cold night sky, I wasn't sure of anything anymore.

As I looked up at the stars, I felt the weight of the world pressing down on me. The responsibilities, the decisions, the lives that depended on me—it was all too much.

And for the first time, I wondered if I had made the wrong choice in coming back.

If maybe I was the one who was destroying everything I had sworn to protect.

Chapter 13

The world was closing in on me.

Every step I took, every breath I drew, felt heavier. I couldn't remember the last time I felt peace—not in my bones, not in my mind. The blood was constant, like a red mist hanging over my vision, obscuring any hope of seeing things clearly. All I could see were the faces of the dead—those who had fallen because of me, trusted me, and would never return.

However, none of that mattered anymore.

What mattered now was power. Control. Vengeance.

I had let the Ferrantis hit us; I had let them wound us. But this time? This time I wasn't playing defense. I was taking everything back, and anyone in my way would fall—family or not.

Ranger was recovering slowly, still weak from his injuries. He hadn't spoken much since the attack, mostly resting and occasionally throwing me a look that said more than words ever could. He knew what I was doing. He was also aware of the direction my actions were taking.

However, I didn't care. I couldn't afford to care anymore.

The estate had grown quieter in recent days. I'd noticed the way people talked less and looked at me less. There were fewer hushed conversations among my men, fewer sideways glances when I entered a room. Fear had settled in. I could feel it in the air, in the way they moved around me—like they were treading carefully, unsure if one wrong word would set me off.

And maybe it would.

I had pushed them hard. Harder than ever. The pace had been relentless, the demands unceasing. Our operations had ramped up, and I expected everyone to keep up and deliver, no matter the cost. They had wanted a leader. They had begged me to return, to take Carlo's place, to restore the family's honor. But what they didn't realize was that I wasn't Carlo. I wasn't the same kind of leader.

Carlo had ruled with power, but he had also ruled with charm. He had known how to make people love him, even as they feared him. But me? I only had a fear. And now, that was starting to feel like the only thing holding everything together.

The call came late in the night.

I was in my study, the dim light casting shadows on the walls as I stared down at the maps and documents scattered across the desk. My head pounded from the hours of planning—the weight of decisions felt like a noose tightening around my neck.

The knock on the door was soft, hesitant.

"Come in," I said, not looking up from the papers.

It was one of the younger men, Luca. His face was pale, his hands fidgeting nervously as he stepped into the room. I could tell from his posture, from the way his eyes wouldn't meet mine, that something was wrong.

"Boss," he said, voice barely above a whisper. "There's been… a situation."

I felt a knot tighten in my stomach, but I kept my expression unreadable. "What kind of situation?"

"There was an attack. One of our outposts. It's bad, Silas."

I stood up slowly, the blood draining from my face. "How bad?"

Luca swallowed hard. "We lost several men. And… and Niko. He was—"

"Niko?" The word felt like a punch to the gut.

He nodded, his eyes dropping to the floor. "He didn't make it."

Niko. My cousin. My blood. One of the few people in this world I still considered family in the truest sense. He had been loyal and dependable, always by my side when I needed him. And now he was gone. Dead, because of me. Because of this war.

The room spun for a moment, my vision narrowing as the reality of it hit me. I had pushed him too far and sent him into a fight he couldn't win. And now he was gone, another casualty in a war that was slowly devouring everything I had left.

I didn't attend the funeral.

I couldn't face it. I couldn't stand to see the grief in my family's eyes; I couldn't bear to hear the whispers and the accusations. They wouldn't say it out loud, but I knew what they were thinking.

This is your fault, Silas. You brought this war to us. You sent Niko to his death.

I stayed at the estate instead, alone in my study, the weight of his death pressing down on me like a crushing wave. I couldn't escape it. Everywhere I turned, there was another reminder of my failure. The faces of the men who had died under my command haunted me—ghosts that followed me from room to room, their eyes accusing, their voices silent but deafening in my ears.

I had wanted power. I had wanted control. And I had gotten it. But at what cost?

Every step I took seemed to bring me closer to the edge, closer to losing myself completely in the violence, in the bloodshed. The lines between right and wrong had blurred long ago, and now I was sinking into the darkness, unable to find my way back.

Ranger found me later that night, his steps slow as he entered the room. He was still recovering, but the fire in his eyes hadn't dimmed. He knew I was spiraling. He had seen it coming long before I had.

"We need to talk," he said, his voice steady.

I didn't look up. "There's nothing to talk about."

"Yes, there is." He stepped closer, his presence commanding my attention whether I wanted to give it or not. "You're pushing them too hard, Silas. The men, the family. They're scared."

"They should be scared," I snapped, my voice colder than I intended. "That's the only way to keep them in line."

Ranger shook his head. "Fear only lasts so long. Eventually, they'll break. Or they'll turn on you."

I looked up at him, my eyes narrowing. "Is that a warning?"

"It's the truth." He didn't flinch and didn't back down. "I know you're hurting. Niko's death—it hit you hard. But you can't keep doing this. You can't keep leading with rage."

"What do you expect me to do?" I shot back, the anger rising in my chest. "Just roll over and let them kill us? Let them take everything."

"No," Ranger said quietly. "But you can't keep sacrificing your own people just to prove a point."

I clenched my fists, my mind racing. I knew he was right, but I couldn't admit it. Not now. Not when everything was falling apart. I had to stay strong. I had to keep pushing, or everything I'd fought for would be lost.

However, deep down, I knew the truth. I was losing myself in the fight, becoming something I never wanted to be.

The days blurred together after that.

I threw myself deeper into the work, into the planning and the fighting. I couldn't think about Niko; I couldn't let myself feel the weight of his death, or it would consume me. I became colder, harder, and more ruthless. The men followed my orders without question, but I could see the fear in their eyes. The respect was fading, replaced by something darker.

I pushed them harder. More attacks, more bloodshed. I needed to remind them who we were and what we stood for. I needed them to fear me more than they feared our enemies.

Still, with every battle, with every life lost, I felt a piece of myself slipping away. The faces of the dead haunted me—Niko, the men who had fallen under my command, the innocents caught in the crossfire. They were all ghosts now, lingering in the corners of my mind, reminding me of what I had lost.

It wasn't until another attack occurred at one of our establishments that I finally broke down.

I had sent a team to deal with a rival family that had been encroaching on our territory. It should have been a simple job. However, they had been prepared for our arrival. Ambushed. The call came in late at night, and by the time we arrived, it was too late.

The place was in ruins. Bodies lay scattered across the ground, blood soaking into the dirt. I stood there, staring at the carnage, feeling the weight of every death pressing down on me. This was my fault. I had sent them here. I had led them into a trap.

One of the men, barely alive, was dragged to my feet. His face was pale, his breathing shallow, but his eyes were filled with something worse than pain—disappointment.

"I'm sorry," he rasped, blood bubbling at his lips. "We tried, but they knew."

I kneeled beside him, my chest tight. "Don't talk. Save your strength."

However, he shook his head, coughing weakly. "It's over, Silas. They're too strong. We... we can't keep doing this."

He died in my arms, his blood staining my hands. Another life lost because of me. Another ghost added to the growing list.

I stood there for what felt like hours, staring down at the body, my mind numb. I had led these men to their deaths. I had promised them victory, promised them that we would win this war, and instead, I had given them nothing but blood and death.

I couldn't keep doing this. I couldn't keep pretending that I was the leader they needed. I wasn't. I was failing them. And I was failing myself.

Back at the estate, I locked myself in my study, the silence deafening. The weight of everything crashed down on me, and for the first time in a long time, I felt tears burning in my eyes.

I had lost Niko. I had lost my men. And now I was losing myself.

I sat there, staring at the maps, the plans, and the endless cycle of violence that had consumed my life. This wasn't what I had wanted. This wasn't the life Lena had dreamed of for us. This wasn't the family I had sworn to protect.

I was becoming a monster. And I didn't know how to stop it.

Ranger found me again, just like before. But this time, he didn't say anything. He didn't need to.

He sat down across from me, his eyes filled with understanding and something I hadn't seen in a long time—compassion. He didn't push me. He didn't try to fix it. He just sat there, letting me feel the weight of everything I had done.

And for the first time in a long time, I didn't feel completely alone.

However, that didn't change the fact that I had a decision to make.

The war wasn't over. And if I wanted to survive, if I wanted to protect what was left of my family, I had to keep fighting.

Still, as I looked into Ranger's eyes, I wondered if I could keep going without losing the last piece of my soul.

Because right now? I wasn't sure if I had anything left to give.

Chapter 14

The name came to me in hushed tones, an old whisper that had lingered in the halls of our family's empire—a familiar echo I hadn't heard in years. Lorenzo Marino. The man had once been a trusted ally, someone who had stood beside my family during some of its darkest times.

We had grown up nearly side by side, each of us learning to navigate the treacherous waters of this world and tethered to its grim realities in ways we hadn't chosen. And now, it seemed, he had become one of the very threats I had sworn to eliminate. It didn't make sense at first. Lorenzo had been a loyal companion, a man who had once sworn that family came before all else. I couldn't believe he had truly turned against us, unless there was some driving force behind it.

I needed answers. I needed to understand why. But getting close to him would be dangerous. He was smart, cunning, and, if what I'd heard was true, more ruthless than ever.

Ranger entered my study, his eyes as sharp as always, though there was an underlying weariness to his gaze that even he couldn't hide. I motioned for him to sit, watching him carefully as he lowered himself into the chair opposite me. I was aware that he shared my sense of weight and the sensation of everything hovering on the brink of collapse. "Lorenzo Marino," I said, the name hanging between us like a phantom. Ranger's expression hardened. He had known Lorenzo as well and had worked alongside him more times than he could count.

"He's after you," Ranger replied, his voice low. "And it's personal." I raised an eyebrow, sensing there was more he wasn't saying.

"What happened between us, Ranger? Why would Lorenzo be targeting my family now?" Ranger hesitated, his jaw tightening as he weighed his words. Finally, he leaned forward, his gaze steady.

"It's not just about you, Silas. It's about what your father did. Carlo made choices—ones that hurt people who were supposed to be friends. Lorenzo's family was one of them."

My stomach twisted. I had always known that his choices had left scars and that his decisions had made us enemies in places I had never even considered. However, hearing that one of those wounds had festered to this level of hatred struck something deep within me.

"What did Carlo do?" I inquired, even though a part of me already knew the answer. "Carlo and Lorenzo's father... there was a disagreement," Ranger explained, choosing his words carefully. "It was over territory and money. The usual. Still, it got messy. People died—people close to Lorenzo. Carlo took what he wanted, and Lorenzo's family was left with nothing but anger and loss." I clenched my fists, feeling a surge of anger mixed with a strange sense of guilt.

Lorenzo's hatred wasn't baseless; it was rooted in the pain my family had caused. And now, he was coming for us, determined to exact the revenge that had been simmering for years. It was both a personal vendetta and a ruthless ambition. Lorenzo wasn't just looking to hurt me—he wanted to dismantle everything my family stood for.

The realization left a bitter taste in my mouth. I had always believed in the strength of my family and in the power of loyalty and legacy. But now, standing at the edge of absolute control, I felt more alone than ever. I had clawed my way back to the top and sacrificed everything to regain what I had lost. And yet, as I looked around, I realized that my pursuit of power had left me isolated—surrounded by fear and mistrust rather than loyalty and love. Ranger's voice broke through my thoughts, pulling me back to the present.

"Silas, if we're going to face Lorenzo, we need a plan—a strong one. This won't be a simple fight. He knows our weaknesses, knows how to hurt us where it matters." I nodded, my mind racing as I considered the possibilities. Confronting Lorenzo head-on would be reckless; he was expecting that. However, if I strategically manipulated his anger, I could potentially reverse the situation.

The plan began to take shape, ominous and methodical, akin to a shadow encroaching on my mental terrain. I would bait him, draw him out, and make him reveal his vulnerabilities. It was dangerous, but it was the only way to dismantle his strength without walking into a trap.

For the next few hours, Ranger and I strategize, discussing every possible angle and every potential move Lorenzo might make. He was a formidable opponent, but he wasn't invincible. His hatred was a weapon, yes, but it was also a weakness—one that I intended to exploit. By the time we were finished, the plan was set—a web of deception and manipulation that would lure Lorenzo into a confrontation he couldn't escape.

As Ranger left to prepare the necessary arrangements, I remained in the study, the weight of what lay ahead pressing down on me like an invisible hand. I had been so focused on securing my family's dominance and reclaiming the power that had once been ours that I hadn't stopped to consider what it was costing me. I had lost friends, allies, even family, all in the name of a legacy that was beginning to feel like a curse. And now, standing on the brink of what could be our final battle, I couldn't shake the feeling that I was standing there alone.

Night fell, and with it came a silence that seemed to amplify the chaos in my mind. I found myself wandering through the empty halls of the estate, my footsteps echoing against the cold stone walls. Everywhere I looked, I saw reminders of the family I once knew—the family I had sacrificed so much to protect. But as I passed the portraits, the mementos of a life I had tried to reclaim, I realized that my family was gone—lost to the violence, to the betrayals, and to the endless cycle of blood and power. This fight with Lorenzo wasn't just about survival; it was about everything I had built, everything I had fought for. And yet, as I stood there, staring at the remnants of a life I could barely recognize, I couldn't help but wonder if anything had been worth it.

The weight of that question settled over me—a cold realization that gnawed at my resolve. I had always believed that power was the answer and that control was the only way to protect what mattered. But now, facing the threat of annihilation from a man who had once been a friend, I was forced to confront the possibility that my pursuit of power had driven away the very people I was trying to protect. A knock on the door broke the silence, and I turned to see Ranger standing in the doorway, his expression grave.

"It's time, Silas," he said, his voice steady but carrying an edge of urgency.

"Lorenzo's forces are mobilizing. We need to move now if we're going to have the upper hand." I nodded, pushing down the lingering doubts as I followed him out of the room. This was it—the final confrontation that would decide everything. There was no turning back now, no room for hesitation. It was a fight for survival, for dominance, for everything my family had built.

The drive to the rendezvous point was tense, the silence between us thick with unspoken fears and uncertainties. Ranger sat beside me, his gaze fixed on the road ahead, his jaw set with determination. He had been my confidant, my friend, and my only ally in this brutal world. And as we neared the location where we would face Lorenzo,

I felt a surge of gratitude for his loyalty and for his willingness to stand by me even when the odds were stacked against us.

When we arrived, the air was charged with anticipation—the quiet tension of men preparing for battle. I could see the fear in their eyes, the uncertainty that lingered just beneath the surface. They were ready to fight, but they knew the risks. They knew that this could be the end.

As we waited for Lorenzo's forces to arrive, I found myself standing alone; the weight of everything I had done and everything I had lost was pressing down on me like a heavy cloak. I had chosen this path—to lead, to fight, and to sacrifice. But now, standing on the edge of absolute control, I realised that I was standing there alone. The thought gnawed at me, a bitter reminder of the cost of power and the isolation that came with it. And yet, despite the doubts and guilt, I knew I couldn't walk away. This was my family, my legacy, and I would protect it, even if it meant sacrificing what little remained of myself.

The sounds of engines approaching broke the silence, pulling me back to the present. Lorenzo's forces were here, the final showdown looming just ahead. I steeled myself, pushing aside the doubts, the guilt, and the loneliness. There was no room for weakness now, no room for hesitation. This was the moment I had fought for, the moment that would decide everything. And as I prepared to face Lorenzo, to confront the man who had once been my friend, I felt a strange sense of calm settle over me.

This was it. The end of the line. And whatever happened next, I was ready.

Chapter 15

The sun barely broke through the thick layer of clouds, casting an oppressive, grey light across the city streets. There was an eerie silence hanging over everything, the kind that settles in the aftermath of something unthinkable. I'd been at the warehouse cleaning up from last night's confrontation when the call came in. Ranger's voice was tight, stripped of its usual calm.

"Silas, you need to see this," he had said, and for the first time since we'd met, I heard something in his voice that I hadn't before— fear.

The address was a small café on the east side of town, one I didn't frequent but had passed a dozen times. The owner, Mr. Pasqual, was a retired teacher known for treating everyone like a friend, a father to every kid in the neighbourhood. As I pulled up, I saw the familiar patrol cars, the yellow crime tape fluttering in the light breeze, and the huddled officers exchanging grim looks. My stomach twisted. This was something I'd been trained to ignore.

Violence and death were inevitable in my world, and usually I could shrug off the toll it took. But this... this felt different.

Ranger was waiting for me by the side entrance, his face unreadable as I walked up. Without a word, he led me inside, past the broken tables and shattered glass, to a scene that was both heartbreaking and all too familiar. There, in the middle of the floor, lay the body of a young woman. She couldn't have been older than twenty-two. Her wide, unseeing eyes stared up at the ceiling, her face frozen in a look of shock. My heart clenched as I took in her appearance—the vibrant red streak in her hair, her jeans, and her oversized sweater—she had likely been on her way to class or a part-time job, unaware of the danger lurking in her city. I felt a hollowness open up inside me—a dark chasm that swallowed all the reasons and justifications that I had clung to.

"She was just in the wrong place at the wrong time," Ranger said softly, his voice barely more than a whisper.

I could barely meet his eyes. "Who?" My voice sounded foreign, cold even to my own ears. I didn't want to know, but at the same time, I needed to know. Who had done this? Who made the decision to target a civilian location like this? Ranger took a deep breath, his jaw clenching as he forced the words out. "Lorenzo's men. They've started pushing outward, hitting places they know you frequent or might. They... they didn't care who was inside."

The truth of it hit me like a punch to the gut. Lorenzo wasn't just after me or my men anymore; he was targeting the very city itself. The people, the places, the innocent lives that had nothing to do with our world—they were all now fair game in his twisted vendetta.

I stared down at the lifeless body, feeling the weight of every decision I'd made piling up on my shoulders, threatening to crush me. This was my fault. I knew it, felt it deep in my bones. My choices, my fight, my pride—this was the price.

The air in the café seemed to grow colder, and I found myself backing away from the scene, desperate for a breath of fresh air, desperate to escape the overwhelming guilt that clawed at me. Outside, the city continued on, blissfully unaware of the darkness that had seeped into its streets. But I knew that the peace was an illusion, a fragile façade that could shatter at any moment. And I was the one holding the hammer. I leaned against the wall, closing my eyes as the weight of it all pressed down on me. This wasn't supposed to happen. I had always told myself that my war was contained, that the collateral damage would be minimal, and that I could control the impact. But now, staring at the cost of my choices, I realised just how naive I had been.

Ranger joined me outside, his expression grim but resolute. "This is escalating, Silas. If we don't do something to end it—if *you* don't do something—it's only going to get worse."

I swallowed, the bitterness of my failure sitting heavy in my chest. I had tried to avoid the guilt, tried to push it aside and justify it as necessary, as inevitable. But today, there was no avoiding it. I couldn't shake the image of that young woman; her life was cut short because of a war she had no part in, a war she probably didn't even know existed. I turned to Ranger, my voice barely more than a whisper. "Maybe... maybe I was wrong to come back. Maybe I should have stayed away; let the family crumble; let them figure it out on their own."

Ranger's gaze hardened. "Don't you dare, Silas. Don't you dare run away again. This is on you, yes, but it's also on Lorenzo, on Carlo, on every single person who's chosen this life. You're not the only one who's made mistakes. You're not the only one who's caused harm."

However, that didn't make it any easier to bear. The guilt twisted inside me, sharp and unrelenting. I had always believed that power was worth the cost and that the legacy I'd inherited was something to be proud of. But now, standing on the edge of a war that had already claimed too many innocent lives, I wasn't so sure. The thought of walking away, of leaving this life behind, tugged at me with an intensity I hadn't felt in years. But I knew, deep down, that it wasn't an option. There was no escaping the shadow of my choices, no erasing the blood on my hands. I could walk away, but the weight of this war would follow me wherever I went. I had chosen this path, and now I had to see it through.

The next few days passed in a blur. I went through the motions, planning our next move, strategizing, and trying to find a way to end this without dragging more lives into the crossfire. But no matter how hard I tried to focus, that young woman's face haunted me, a constant reminder of the cost of my choices. I barely slept, barely ate, the guilt gnawing at me with every passing hour. Ranger noticed, of course. He always did. But he didn't push me; he didn't force me to confront it. Instead, he stayed by my side, his quiet presence a small comfort in the midst of the storm.

Finally, I couldn't take it anymore. One night, as the city lay quiet and still, I found myself back at the café. The scene had been cleaned up, the broken glass swept away, and the tables rearranged as if nothing had ever happened. But the emptiness lingered, a hollow echo of the life that had been lost. I sat down at one of the tables, the silence pressing in around me. For the first time, I allowed myself to feel the full weight of my actions and to confront the guilt and the regret that I had been avoiding. I thought about the people who had died because of me, the lives that had been shattered, the families who would never be whole again. And I wondered if any of it was worth it.

I had always believed that power was the answer and that control was the only way to protect what mattered. But now, sitting alone in the darkness, I wasn't so sure. I felt hollow, empty, as if the very essence of who I was had been stripped away, leaving nothing but a shell of the man I used to be. And for the first time, I felt a surge of doubt, a gnawing fear that maybe I wasn't cut out for this, that maybe I wasn't the leader my family needed.

In that quiet moment, I felt the urge to walk away again, to leave it all behind and disappear into the shadows. But as tempting as it was, I knew it was an illusion, a fleeting escape that would solve nothing. Running wouldn't bring back the lives that had been lost; it wouldn't undo the damage that had been done. It would only add to the guilt, the shame, and the emptiness that had consumed me.

As I sat there, staring into the darkness, a strange sense of calm settled over me. I realised, with a clarity that was both painful and freeing, that there was no escaping this life. I was bound to it, tied to its darkness and its blood. And as much as I hated it, as much as I wished I could turn back time and choose a different path, I knew that I couldn't. The weight of this legacy, this power, was mine to bear. And I would carry it, no matter the cost.

I stood up, the quiet resolve settling over me like a second skin. There was no turning back now. The war would continue, the bloodshed would go on, and I would be there, leading my family, protecting what was left. It wasn't a choice—it was a duty, a burden that I had inherited, a destiny that I couldn't escape.

As I walked out of the café and into the darkened streets, I felt a strange sense of peace. The guilt was still there, the regret lingering like a shadow. However, for the first time, I accepted it and embraced it as part of who I was. I was Silas, the head of this family, the bearer of its legacy. And I would see it through, no matter the cost.

Chapter 16

I'd always known that everyone in my world carried secrets. I had my own—deep, dark ones that I hoped would die with me. However, lately, I had started to realise that the people around me had secrets too, ones I hadn't bothered to notice before. Ranger, in particular, had more secrets than he shared.

Ranger stood across from me in the dim light of the warehouse, his arms crossed, his expression unreadable as always. We had just finished planning another attack, another desperate push to cripple our enemies. But there was something different in the air tonight. A tension had been building between us for weeks, ever since I started sensing that he wasn't telling me everything. And now, after everything we'd been through—all the battles and the bloodshed—I couldn't shake the feeling that there was more to him than I had ever realized.

I took a step closer, my eyes locking onto his. "You've been holding out on me, Ranger. There's something you're not telling me." My voice was calm, but beneath the surface, anger simmered. I didn't like being kept in the dark—not by anyone, and especially not by the one person I trusted to stand by my side. Ranger didn't flinch; he didn't break eye contact. He was always calm under pressure, but tonight there was something in his eyes—a flicker of something I couldn't quite place. Was it fear? Guilt? He remained silent for a moment, and I could feel the tension thickening between us, like the calm before a storm.

"What makes you think I'm hiding something?" His voice was low, cautious.

I clenched my jaw. "I know you, Ranger. You're always two steps ahead. Always seeing things I don't. But lately, you've been... different. You're not telling me everything, and it's pissing me off."

He didn't respond right away, just stood there, staring at me with that same impassive look that he always wore when he didn't want me to see what he was really thinking. But tonight, I wasn't going to let him shut me out.

"Tell me what's going on," I pressed, stepping closer, my voice hardening. "I don't have time for games. Not now."

Ranger sighed, running a hand through his dark hair before finally speaking. "You're right," he said quietly. "I haven't told you everything. But it's not because I don't trust you, Silas. It's because I wasn't sure if you could handle the truth."

My anger flared. "Handle it? You think I can't handle the truth? After everything we've been through?"

Ranger's eyes flickered with something—regret, maybe—but he didn't back down. "You've been walking a fine line, Silas. Ever since you came back, you've been trying to hold onto your humanity, trying to lead this family without becoming the monster you fear. But you're losing that fight. And if I told you everything I know, I was afraid you'd tip over the edge."

I stared at him, my heart pounding in my chest. I felt the urge to strike, yell, and insist that he clarify his words. But instead, I forced myself to stay calm, to breathe through the rage that was building inside me.

"Tell me," I said, my voice dangerously low. "Now."

Ranger took a step forward, his eyes locked onto mine. "Fine. But you're not going to like it."

For the first time, I saw hesitation in his gaze—a crack in the armor of his usual stoicism. It only made me more anxious.

"You want to know why Lorenzo's been escalating his attacks?" he asked. "Why is he so determined to wipe us out?"

I nodded. "Obviously."

Ranger's eyes darkened, and for a moment, I thought he might not say it. But then the words spilt out, each one landing like a blow.

"Because Carlo made a deal with him. This deal was made a long time ago, even before you joined the group. Carlo promised Lorenzo control of half the territory in exchange for his help in taking down another rival family. But when you took over, that deal was... forgotten."

My chest tightened. "What are you saying?"

Ranger shook his head, his voice softening. "I'm saying that the reason this war is spiraling out of control is because of a deal your father made—one that was never onored. And now, Lorenzo's trying to collect."

The impact of his words struck me deeply. I staggered back, unable to process what he was telling me. My father had made deals with the enemy. He had sold out part of our family's empire to Lorenzo. And now, because I had stepped in—because I hadn't honored the deal that I didn't even know existed—we were paying the price?

"I didn't know," I said, my voice barely more than a whisper. "How could I have known?"

Ranger's expression softened slightly, but the tension between us was still thick. "I know you didn't know. Yet Lorenzo still sees you as the one who broke the agreement. He sees you as the reason everything is falling apart."

I clenched my fists, the anger rising again. "So why didn't you tell me this sooner? Why the hell did you keep this from me?"

Ranger's gaze didn't waver. "Because I didn't think you were ready to hear it. You've been struggling to lead, Silas. You've struggled to balance family and your ideal self. And I didn't want to throw this on you when you were already falling apart."

My hands shook with fury, but beneath that, I felt something else—betrayal. Ranger had been the one person I trusted and thought I could rely on. And now I was finding out that he'd been keeping secrets from me, hiding things that could have changed everything.

I took a step closer to him, my voice trembling with barely controlled rage. "You should have told me. I don't care if you thought I wasn't ready. I needed to know."

Ranger held my gaze, his expression grim. "And what would you have done if I had told you sooner? You would've spiralled, Silas. You would've pushed yourself even harder, tried to take everything on your shoulders, and it would've destroyed you."

I wanted to argue, to fight back, but the truth of his words settled in my chest like a weight. He was right. For weeks, I had been in a precarious situation, barely managing to hold myself together. This revelation about my father and Lorenzo might have finally pushed me over the edge.

Still, that didn't make it easier to accept. It didn't erase the anger or the feeling of betrayal.

"I trusted you," I whispered, the words slipping out before I could stop them.

Ranger's face softened, and for the first time, I saw a hint of vulnerability in his eyes. "I know. And I'm still here, Silas. I've always been here. But sometimes, leading means making decisions that others won't understand. It's not about secrets—it's about survival."

For a long moment, neither of us spoke. The silence between us stretched, filled with everything that hadn't been said. In that silence, I realized something. Ranger wasn't just trying to protect me—he was trying to save me from myself.

I looked away, my anger deflating as exhaustion settled in. I was so damn tired. I was weary of battling, weary of the violence, and weary of everything pressing down upon me.

"I don't know if I can do this," I admitted, the words tasting bitter on my tongue. "I don't know if I can lead this family. Every decision I make leads to the death of innocent people. Innocent people. And now, with this..."

Ranger's hand landed on my shoulder, solid and steady. "You can do this. You've already done it. However, you must cease attempting to handle everything alone. That's why I'm here. That's why your family is here. We're in this together, Silas."

His words hit me harder than I expected. Together. It felt foreign to me—the idea of sharing the burden, of trusting others with the weight that had always felt like mine alone. But as I stood there, staring at the man who had become not just an ally but a friend, I realised that I couldn't do this without him. I couldn't do this without them.

I nodded slowly, the tension between us easing just slightly. "I'm sorry," I said quietly. "For not trusting you."

Ranger offered a small, almost sad smile. "It's not about trust, Silas. It's about survival. We've both done what we had to do to survive. We must accomplish more than survive to win this war. We need to trust each other."

I met his gaze, feeling the truth of his words settle in. He was right. We couldn't afford to keep secrets, to let fear and doubt tear us apart. To defeat Lorenzo and save my family, we had to work together.

"Alright," I said, the word feeling like a decision, like a promise. "No more secrets. We do this together."

Ranger nodded, his expression serious. "Together."

For the first time in what felt like weeks, I felt a spark of hope flicker inside me. It wasn't much, but it was enough to remind me that I wasn't alone in this. Regardless of the depths of darkness, I had support from those around me. They had faith in me, despite my lack of self-belief.

"Now," Ranger said, his voice turning brisk, "we need to figure out our next move. Lorenzo's getting desperate, but that also means he's dangerous. If we're going to take him down, we need to be smart about it."

I nodded, the weight of the conversation lifting slightly as we turned our focus back to the war at hand. There was still so much to do, so many battles ahead. But for the first time, I felt like we might actually have a chance.

We spent the next few hours going over our plans, refining our strategies, and preparing for the final push. Ranger was methodical, his mind sharp as ever, but there was a new tension between us, a new layer of understanding that hadn't been there before. We didn't need to talk about it—it was just there, unspoken but present.

As the night wore on and the weight of exhaustion settled in, I found myself reflecting on everything that had happened. The secrets, the betrayals, the bloodshed. However, we also cherished the bonds, trust, and connections we had established between us.

For the first time in a long time, I felt a strange sense of peace. Not because the war was over—not by a long shot—but because I knew that, no matter what happened, I wasn't in this fight alone.

Ranger's voice cut through my thoughts. "We're ready, Silas. Whatever happens next, we'll be ready."

I nodded, feeling the truth of his words settle deep inside me. "Yeah," I said quietly, my voice steady. "We're ready."

Chapter 17

The night was thick with tension, a pressure that weighed down on every breath and every heartbeat. The last few days had been a whirlwind of preparation, every member of the family scrambling to prepare themselves for the final assault against Lorenzo's clan. This was it—the battle that would determine everything. Either we'd leave victorious, stronger than ever, or we'd collapse under the weight of failure, our family shattered beyond repair. As I looked around the room at the faces of those who had chosen to follow me, some out of loyalty, some out of fear, I couldn't ignore the knot twisting inside my gut. They trusted me to lead them into battle and ensure their survival.

Ranger stepped up beside me, his gaze fixed on the map we'd laid out on the table. We'd spent hours poring over every detail, examining every possible angle. Still, doubts lingered, shadows lurking in the corners of my mind. Ranger's voice broke through my thoughts, steady and calm. "We've planned for everything, Silas. You've done everything you can."

I nodded, but his words did little to settle the storm brewing inside me. The truth was, I hadn't stopped questioning this plan since we put it in motion. I'd told myself a thousand times that this was necessary and that Lorenzo had given me no other choice. But as the moment approached, I felt the weight of every decision I'd made pressing down on me, like a lead blanket smothering my conviction.

The plan was simple, but the stakes were brutal. We'd split into two groups: one would draw Lorenzo's men into an ambush, while the second would strike from behind, cutting them down in a single, decisive move. We knew their weak points; we'd spent days scouting their hideouts, tracking their routines. There was no room for hesitation, no margin for error. And yet, I couldn't shake the thought that something was bound to go wrong. It always did.

The silence in the room grew heavier as the minutes ticked by. Ranger glanced at me; his eyes narrowed, as if he could see right through the mask I'd carefully put on. "You're doubting this," he said quietly, his voice a mix of curiosity and concern.

I took a deep breath, knowing I couldn't hide it. Not from him. "I just keep thinking... we're about to spill a lot of blood tonight. And for what? To prove we're stronger? To keep this family alive? At what point does survival become a question of how much we're willing to lose?"

Ranger's gaze hardened, and for a moment, I saw a flicker of something raw and unfiltered in his expression. "Silas, if you're having doubts now, you need to push them aside. You know this isn't just about survival. Lorenzo's been pushing us to this point for months. He's threatened everything and everyone you care about. If you hesitate now, we'll all pay the price."

He was right. I knew he was. But that didn't make it any easier to accept. I could sense the weight of every life in peril, each individual poised to engage in a conflict that could potentially lead to the end of everything. The worst part was that I wasn't sure I could handle the consequences if I failed them.

With a deep breath, I pushed the doubts aside, forcing myself to focus on the plan and on the steps we'd laid out, each one leading us closer to the moment that would decide our fate. I looked at Ranger, nodding. "You're right. Let's do this."

The night air was cool and sharp as we moved into position, the darkness blanketing us as we waited for the signal. My pulse thundered in my ears, every muscle tensed, my senses on high alert. We'd positioned ourselves just outside the main hideout where Lorenzo's men were stationed, a crumbling warehouse that sat on the outskirts of town. My team was in place, scattered around the perimeter, waiting for the signal. Ranger was across from me, his expression hard, his gaze fixed on the target.

As the seconds stretched into minutes, I felt a strange calm settle over me, a cold clarity that came with the knowledge that there was no turning back. This was it. The final gamble. Do or die.

The signal came—a faint click over the radio. I raised my hand, signaling for the men to move. Like shadows, we advanced toward the building, slipping through the darkness with silent precision. We reached the entrance, and I could hear the muffled voices of Lorenzo's men inside, laughing, unaware of the storm about to break over them.

With a nod to Ranger, I kicked open the door, and chaos erupted.

The room exploded into a frenzy of gunfire, the deafening roar of bullets filling the air as we charged in, each shot landing with deadly accuracy. Lorenzo's men scrambled, taken by surprise, some barely managing to draw their weapons before they were cut down. My heart raced, every sense heightened as I moved through the chaos, focused and unyielding. I could see Ranger beside me, his movements sharp and efficient, cutting down anyone who dared to stand in our way.

For a moment, it seemed like we were winning, like victory was within reach. But then, out of the corner of my eye, I saw something that made my blood run cold—a civilian caught in the crossfire, clutching a young child to her chest, her eyes wide with terror. She hadn't been part of the plan. None of this had been meant for her. I froze, my gun halfway raised. A sickening realization settled over me.

This was the cost. This innocent life, this terrified family—they were the ones paying for my war, my need for power, my decision to retaliate. And in that moment, as I stood there, watching the fear in her eyes, I felt a crack open up inside me—a fracture in the armor I'd built around my heart.

I didn't have time to process it, didn't have time to act, because in the next instant, I was forced to duck as a bullet whizzed past my head, snapping me back to the reality of the fight. I moved on instinct, firing back, my focus narrowing to the immediate threat. But the image of that woman and her child stayed with me, haunting me with every step and every shot.

As the fight raged on, I could feel something inside me shifting—a realization settling over me like a heavy weight. This was more than a fight for survival. This was a war that was tearing me apart, that was turning me into something I could barely recognise.

In the heat of the battle, I made my way through the chaos, my gaze searching for Lorenzo. He was the reason we were here, the reason all of this was happening. If I could end him, maybe I could finally put an end to this nightmare. But as I moved, my thoughts drifted back to that woman, to the fear in her eyes, and I felt a pang of guilt twist in my chest.

Finally, I saw him—Lorenzo, standing at the far end of the room, his back against the wall, a look of defiance in his eyes. He raised his gun, aiming it directly at me, and for a brief moment, everything else faded away. It was just the two of us, locked in a deadly standoff.

I raised my gun, my hand steady, my gaze fixed on him. But as I looked into his eyes, I felt a flicker of hesitation, a whisper of doubt that cut through the adrenaline-fuelled haze.

This was it. This was the moment I'd been fighting for, the victory I'd been willing to sacrifice everything to achieve. But now, as I stood there, on the brink of victory, I couldn't shake the feeling that the cost was too high. The loss of something far more valuable than power or control was imminent.

For a brief moment, I couldn't determine who had fired the gun. But then I saw Lorenzo slump to the ground, the light fading from his eyes, and I knew that it was over. The fight, the war, everything—it was done.

The silence that followed was deafening—a hollow emptiness that echoed through the room, settling over me like a shroud. I looked around at the bodies strewn across the floor, at the blood that stained the walls, and felt a wave of exhaustion wash over me, a bone-deep weariness that left me hollow and numb.

Ranger stepped up beside me, his gaze flicking between me and the carnage around us. He didn't say anything, didn't offer any words of comfort or congratulations. He just stood there, his presence a steady anchor in the storm of emotions that churned inside me.

I looked at him, the weight of everything settling over me like a crushing burden. "Was it worth it?" I asked, my voice barely more than a whisper.

Ranger met my gaze, his expression unreadable. "Only you can answer that, Silas."

I nodded, the truth of his words weighing heavily on me. This was the cost of power, of loyalty, of family. And as I stood there, surrounded by the wreckage of everything I'd fought for, I realized that maybe—just maybe—it wasn't worth it after all.

The war was over, but the price... the price was something I would carry with me for the rest of my life.

Chapter 18

Post-battle silence was more oppressive than noise. I stood among the wreckage, surrounded by the fallen—our enemies, our men—each of them lost in the name of securing our family's power. The ground beneath me was stained with blood—a mix of crimson that no one could separate into friends or foes. It was just blood. And we had paid for this victory in gallons.

My hands trembled as I wiped the sweat from my brow, and my mind clouded with exhaustion and a hollow sense of accomplishment. It was over—Lorenzo was dead, his clan shattered. The enemy we had spent so much time planning to destroy was now a memory, buried in the ashes of this battle. But instead of the satisfaction I thought I'd feel, all I could focus on was the bodies, the broken pieces of lives I'd sacrificed along the way. The faces of those who trusted me, who had followed me into this hell, haunted me.

Some of them had been with me from the beginning; others had been strangers when this war started. But now, they were all the same—gone, their lives spent in service to a goal I wasn't even sure was worth it anymore.

I looked around for Ranger, needing to ground myself and hear something that would make sense of all this. He was standing a few feet away, leaning against the side of a wrecked car, his breathing ragged but steady. He'd been wounded in the fight, though not severely, and despite the chaos swirling around us, he was calm, his eyes distant, lost in thought.

As I approached him, he turned his gaze toward me, his expression unreadable. "We did it," I said, the words sounding empty even as they left my mouth.

Ranger didn't respond immediately. He just stared at me, his eyes darker than I'd ever seen them. Finally, he spoke, his voice low, almost a whisper. "You think it's over?"

I frowned, not understanding. "Lorenzo's dead. His clan is in ruins. We've won."

Ranger shook his head slowly, a grim smile tugging at the corner of his mouth. "This was never about winning, Silas. Not really."

I felt a chill crawl down my spine. "What are you talking about?"

He pushed himself off the car, wincing as he straightened up, his hand pressing against his side where a bullet had grazed him. "You've been fighting this war like you could end it. Like wiping out Lorenzo's clan would somehow put a stop to everything. But that's not how this works. It never was."

My pulse quickened, a cold sweat breaking out on my skin. "Then what the hell was this for? All the bloodshed, all the sacrifices— what was the point?"

Ranger's eyes bore into mine, filled with a mix of pity and something far darker. "The point, Silas, is that there's no end. This is how it's always been. You think Lorenzo was the first? You think our family hasn't done this before, hasn't wiped out clans, and hasn't been wiped out in return? You've been caught in a cycle—the same one your father was in, the same one his father was in before him. And you didn't even see it."

My breath caught in my throat. "What are you saying?"

Ranger took a step closer, his voice dropping even lower. "I'm saying this is how it always goes. We rise, we fall. We kill, we get killed. Power shifts, blood is spilt, and nothing really changes. Lorenzo's gone, sure. But there's always another. Always another enemy, always another fight. The only difference is how much you're willing to sacrifice to stay on top."

I stared at him, my heart pounding in my chest, my mind spinning. "So, what? You're telling me this was all for nothing?"

Ranger's grim smile returned. "I'm telling you it's never for nothing, but it's never enough. You secured the family's power, yes. But at what cost? Look around you, Silas. Look at what's left."

I didn't want to look. I didn't want to see the bodies; I didn't want to feel the weight of every life lost in my quest for control. But I couldn't avoid it. The faces of the dead flashed before my eyes— men who had trusted me, who had fought for me. The woman I had helped is now a pawn in a world I could never escape. Even Ranger, who had stood by my side through all of this, was carrying wounds—some physical, others far deeper. And then there was me. Standing here, victorious but broken, hollowed out by the sacrifices I'd made. By the man I'd become.

Ranger's voice softened, his tone almost compassionate. "This is the cost of leadership, Silas. Of power. You can't escape it. Regardless of your desire to do so, you cannot escape it. No matter how much you fight against it. This is your life now. This is who you are."

I shook my head, stepping back, the weight of his words crashing down on me. "I didn't want this. I never wanted this."

Ranger's eyes hardened, his voice cutting through the air like a blade. "But you took it. You stepped into this role, and now you're in it. And there's no getting out."

The realisation hit me like a freight train. This was my life. The endless cycle of violence, the bloodshed, the loss—it would never end. I had fought so hard to secure my family's place, to protect what was mine, but in doing so, I had trapped myself in a prison of my own making. There was no escape. Not for me. Not for anyone in this life.

I looked out over the battlefield, at the destruction and the chaos, and felt the weight of my decisions press down on me like a crushing force. The battle was over, but the war—the war would never end. Not for me. Not for my family.

Ranger stepped beside me, his voice quiet but steady. "You can't run from this, Silas. You never could."

He was right. Deep down, I'd known it all along. No matter how far I ran, no matter how hard I fought, the shadow of my past would always follow me. I was born into this life, and I would die in it.

I turned to Ranger, my voice barely more than a whisper. "What now?"

Ranger met my gaze, his expression unreadable. "Now? Now, we rebuild. We prepare for what comes next. Because there's always something coming, Silas. Always."

His words hung in the air, heavy and foreboding. I knew he was right. The victory we had won today would only buy us time. Time to regroup, time to recover. But eventually, the cycle would start again. Another enemy, another battle, another sacrifice. It was inevitable.

In the distance, dawn was breaking through the darkness. It was a new day, but it didn't feel like a fresh start. It felt like the continuation of a story that had been playing out for generations—a story I was now part of.

And as I stood there, surrounded by the wreckage of the life I had built, I realized that I couldn't escape it. I couldn't outrun the shadows of my past. They were a part of me, as much a part of me as my blood, my name.

This was my destiny.

However, for the first time, I wasn't sure if I wanted it.

The sun crept higher in the sky, casting long shadows over the battlefield. And as I looked out over the devastation—the bodies, the blood—I knew one thing for certain:

The war wasn't over.

It had only just begun.

"Why do we learn history?

It shall not repeat.

Still, it does..."

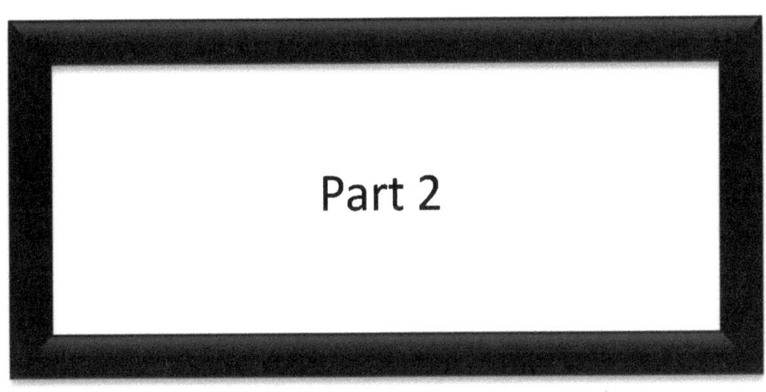
Part 2

Chapter 1

Seven years. Seven years since I'd clawed this family back from the edge of destruction, building its strength on the foundation of blood and loyalty. Seven years, and yet here I was, looking around the room and feeling only the cracks I'd never seen before. Power clung to me, but there was a new weight with it, something closer to doubt, as though every inch I'd gained had come at a cost I couldn't fully count.

Ranger was there, as he'd been since the beginning. He'd stood by me through every dark hour, every hard-won battle, and was the closest thing to family I'd allowed myself to have since I'd taken the reins. But something had shifted in him. Ranger had married Leah five years ago—a decision I'd supported on the surface but felt wary of deep down. Her presence had altered the dynamic, whether he realized it or not. It was subtle at first, but undeniable: Ranger was still loyal, yet there was a softness in him, a spark of… peace. And in our world, peace was a liability.

Leah was a woman who understood power. She held it in a way that was unsettling, the kind of strength that turned heads and commanded rooms without needing to say a word. And she reminded me, far too closely, of my mother. The same calm, the same knowing look that seemed to promise both safety and steel. The men respected her, almost to the point of reverence. Ranger, too, had changed in her orbit, his loyalty now extending beyond me, beyond the family, to her. It unnerved me; every day that passed, I watched her influence grow over him.

"Ranger," I said, not bothering to soften my tone. "Things have shifted in the family. We've expanded, we've brought in fresh blood—but this influence Leah has… you've seen it. The way she's shaping things."

Ranger didn't look up immediately. He closed the folder in front of him, pressing his fingers against it as though he was choosing each word with care. "Leah has her strengths, Silas. She's helped stabilize things in ways only she can."

"Helped?" I cut in, feeling the word turn sharp in my mouth. "Or… softened? Look, I trust Leah, but family isn't about kindness or balance, it's about power. Her influence could end up clouding your loyalty, Ranger."

A tension rippled across his face, but he held his ground. "Silas, I don't see peace as weakness. Leah has given me perspective, and maybe that's exactly what the family needs." His voice grew quieter. "Maybe we don't have to be exactly what our fathers were."

The implication sat between us, thick and biting. Ranger's words held a hint of defiance I hadn't heard before. His loyalty had always been steady, unquestioning. But love for Leah had twisted it, softened it, perhaps beyond repair. Loyalty that depended on family could be broken as easily as it was bound; I'd learned that lesson too well. I'd watched my own parents' loyalty collapse under pressure, leaving me to rebuild the pieces alone.

I pushed the conversation back to business, masking the unease that gnawed at me. "I want you to handle the Estevez group. They've pushed back too many times. It's time they remember who holds the power here."

He didn't waver, nodding as the determination I recognized reappeared, even if fleetingly. Ranger was still strong, still capable, but there was a new fragility within him, and I couldn't ignore it. Not with what was at stake.

For days, I kept a close watch, noting every hesitation, every soft word he offered Leah, feeling something dark and familiar rise within me. Her presence was an infection, I could feel it—mild at first, like a fever, but threatening to undermine everything I'd built if left unchecked. I hadn't fought through years of violence and betrayal to lose control now, not because of her.

One evening, I made my way to the far wing of the estate, where Leah had gathered some of the younger men. Her influence had taken hold even in them; I could see it in their eyes, the quiet respect, the subtle admiration. She was kind to them, speaking in a way that none of us did, making them feel valued, seen. She was dangerous.

"Silas," Leah greeted me with a smile when she noticed me at the door. "Didn't think you'd come. It's not your usual scene, is it?"

The men went quiet, and I could feel the shift in the room. They looked to Leah, waiting for her reaction, her approval. Her influence had penetrated deeply, embedding her sway into the very heart of the family.

"No," I replied, keeping my tone even. "I just wanted to remind you to keep your influence... subtle. We don't need distractions."

Her face remained calm, but there was a sharpness in her eyes that reminded me, irritatingly, of my mother's. "Silas, I know my role here. But influence—well, it's not only yours to control."

The words struck deeper than any insult might have. She was right, of course. I could see the effect she had on the men, her capacity to soothe them, to nurture them into a devotion I'd never attempted. But it was a devotion that didn't align with the iron loyalty I'd forged. Her approach was dangerous. The men could become soft, lulled into complacency, and that could cost us everything.

"Ranger may trust you," I warned, lowering my voice, "but don't forget who runs this family. I built it from nothing and I'll protect it with everything I have."

Leah met my gaze without flinching, almost pitying. "Power alone doesn't make a family, Silas," she replied, a quiet sadness in her tone. "It keeps it together, yes, but it can also destroy it."

Her words lingered in the quiet room, each syllable sticking like barbs long after I'd left. I'd never been one to flinch in the face of conflict, but her words stung. I had made power my gospel, my one unbreakable law. But Leah had challenged that in a way I couldn't ignore.

In the days that followed, I began to watch Ranger more closely. I watched for any sign, any shift that would confirm my suspicions. I noted the way he spoke to her, the softening in his gaze, and the growing influence she had over him. Ranger was still ruthless, still effective when necessary, but there was a flicker of something else, something gentler, and it only served to harden my resolve.

One night, after hours of pacing, I found myself sitting alone in my study, a glass of whiskey in hand, the silence weighing heavily around me. Leah's words echoed in my head, unrelenting, challenging everything I'd dedicated my life to. I'd sacrificed my humanity, my peace, for the power that held this family together. Could I have made different choices? Was there a future without this bloodshed?

The thought teased me, twisting itself around my mind, but I knew better. Peace was an illusion, a fragile thing that broke under pressure. I had seen it shatter in my father's hands, had watched him crumble because of love, of weakness. No, my path was clear, unbreakable, and I would never let that softness pollute the family again.

Yet the fear remained, a tight knot of suspicion coiled around my heart. I was no fool; Ranger's loyalty was no longer mine alone. He was slipping, and Leah's influence had only magnified that. If I wanted to keep control, I had to act.

One evening, I saw Ranger and Leah talking quietly in one of the corridors, her hand resting on his arm as she spoke to him in that soothing voice. A flicker of something warm passed between them, a look so familiar that it ignited something in me, some dark, possessive instinct that had nothing to do with jealousy and everything to do with power. She'd changed him, softened him in a way that might destroy us all.

I walked away, my mind racing with possibilities, strategies. If I wanted to save the family, to keep it from crumbling under this new, fragile influence, I had to do more than watch. I would have to remind them both of what lay at the heart of the family, the brutal and uncompromising power I'd wielded to keep us intact.

Late that night, alone in my study, I made my choice. Ranger's love for Leah had made him vulnerable. Her influence, her strength, it all pointed to one conclusion: power would never belong solely to me as long as she remained. I couldn't change Ranger's heart, but I could remind him, as I had done many times before, who held control, and what that control demanded.

The price would be high, but I was prepared. I would see the family secured, no matter the cost, no matter who had to fall. There was no space for weakness in the empire I'd built, no space for love, or peace, or anything but loyalty driven by fear and respect.

The dawn broke through the window, casting its cold light over the study, and I stood, resolved and alone. This was my legacy, and I would ensure its survival—whether Ranger and Leah understood that or not. The family would remain intact, under my rule, bound by the power I'd forged from blood and sacrifice. And if that meant sacrificing them both, so be it. The family came first. Always.

Chapter 2

Leah's influence over the family was undeniable. As soon as she entered our world, a subtle shift in the atmosphere began to permeate my being. She had this way of seeing people, of disarming them with a look or a word, a gentle reminder that they were something more than muscle and firepower. The men responded to her, drawn to her strength in a way that distinguished her from others. For the first time, there was a woman among us who was not merely a wife or a sister. She was someone of her own weight and authority. I'd thought I was prepared for it, but in truth, I hadn't fully understood the cost.

Ranger, my closest ally, my right-hand man, had always been unwavering. Yet now, with Leah by his side, I could see a difference. There was a softness to him that hadn't been there before. He still carried out his duties with the same resolve and still kept his loyalty to the family as solid as ever. But something had shifted, like an anchor loosening in the tide. I saw it in his decisions—the way he spoke with the men, the way he looked to Leah for reassurance, as if her presence alone validated his choices.

The family, though still bound by the same rules, was beginning to adapt around Leah's presence. She was nothing like anyone I'd expected in our world. Where others used force, Leah used persuasion; where others wielded fear, Leah wielded compassion, and it worked. The men respected her, sometimes even looking to her as they would to me, their boss. I couldn't deny her strength and her influence, and in any other situation, I might have admired it. However, in this particular situation, her strength and influence only sparked a renewed sense of caution within me. Leah's influence risked diluting the very strength I had fought so hard to secure.

One afternoon, I watched her in the gardens with a few of the younger men. They gathered around her as she laughed, sharing stories, her eyes alight with something warm and genuine. She reminded me, too painfully, of my mother. And I knew that in our world, softness only invited ruin.

Later that evening, Ranger joined me in the study. He looked exhausted but calm—a satisfaction in his eyes that I recognized and could only attribute to Leah. She was changing him, and every day, I could feel him slipping, the tension between duty and love gnawing at the foundation of his loyalty. I decided to confront it.

"She has quite an effect on you," I remarked, keeping my voice measured.

Ranger didn't flinch. "She's given me peace, Silas. And maybe that's something this family has been missing."

I shook my head; a tight smile formed as I watched him. "Peace, Ranger, has never been part of this family. Peace leads to complacency, and complacency is what kills. I don't think you realize how her presence has altered you. And this family can't afford change."

Ranger leaned forward, a fire in his eyes that reminded me of myself in younger years. "She hasn't made me weak, Silas. If anything, she's made me stronger. A different kind of strength, but strength nonetheless."

His words hung in the air, challenging everything I'd held to be true. But I knew better. Ranger's strength, the one that I relied on, wasn't the kind that flourished in peace. It was built on fire—in the grit and resilience that came from hardship and bloodshed. Leah was gently smoothing away those edges, softening him in a way that I couldn't tolerate.

That night, I barely slept. The family needed to be led with precision and ruthlessness. Yet here we were, under the influence of a force that was subtly, insidiously unravelling our structure. And as much as I hated to admit it, I admired her ability to do it. Leah was more formidable than I'd anticipated, and that made her dangerous.

The weeks slipped by, Leah's presence only growing stronger, more embedded into the very veins of the family. She wasn't like any of the women I'd known—she didn't try to control Ranger or take anything by force. Instead, she understood his instincts, encouraged his humanity, and reminded him of the life he could have beyond the violence. And he listened, not in defiance of me but in a way that planted a seed of conflict deep within him. He was torn, as if part of him wanted to leave the darkness behind but knew he couldn't abandon his loyalty to me.

Then, one evening, I overheard her talking with one of the younger men, Luca. "The family is important, but there's more to life than power," she said softly, almost like a confession. I watched them from the shadows, my fists clenched, a cold realisation settling over me.

She was pregnant. The way she moved, the way she spoke with this quiet, grounded energy—it was clear. And Ranger, he must have known, too. A new life, a child, was coming into this world. I could feel it stirring in the air—a weight that was both promising and terrifying. For Ranger, this child would mean the world, but for me, it meant only one thing: danger. Leah's maternal influence would solidify the bond she had with Ranger and further erode the loyalty that was supposed to be mine.

In that moment, I knew I couldn't let this continue. I couldn't afford to let Leah's influence expand any further. If she survived childbirth, she would shape this child into someone who would one day wield her compassion, her softness—and that was something the family could not survive. I needed an heir who understood power, who understood the harsh world we'd built, not one tempered by a mother's love.

The answer was as clear as it was ruthless. Just as my own father had, I would have to make a choice to secure the family's future. I had seen where weakness could take us; I had watched my own mother's softness bring my father to ruin. I couldn't allow history to repeat itself.

The plan took shape in my mind over the following days, grim and calculated. I knew I'd need the doctor's cooperation, someone I could trust to carry out my intentions without question. Leah was strong, yes, but childbirth was dangerous, and there were ways to ensure a difficult delivery. I'd make it appear natural—a complication that couldn't be prevented.

Ranger would grieve, but he'd recover. The child would survive, shaped by our world and moulded into the image of strength. Leah's influence would end, her softness silenced before it could take root any deeper.

The next day, I arranged to meet with Dr. Evans, our trusted family physician. He was an old man, his hands steady, his loyalty unquestioning. As I explained what I needed, his eyes flickered with the faintest hint of uncertainty, but he nodded, keeping his expression blank.

"It's necessary, Doctor," I told him, my tone leaving no room for argument. "For the good of the family. Leah can't remain—her influence would undermine everything we've built."

He hesitated only a moment before nodding. "I understand, Silas. But know that this will weigh heavily. Once it's done, there's no going back."

"I know," I replied, my voice cold, unyielding. "But it's a price I'm willing to pay."

As the weeks crept closer to Leah's due date, I watched her with a new intensity, every laugh, every gentle touch she shared with

Ranger only solidifying my resolve. Ranger had no idea what was coming, and I'd ensure that he never would. This was for the future of the family, a decision that would ensure our strength for generations.

And yet, as I looked at her one evening, the weight of my choice pressed down on me. I saw the future she could give Ranger, the peace she offered him, and I knew it was a future that would shatter the family's foundation. This was not a family that could thrive on compassion; we were forged in blood and hardened by survival. It was a legacy I would ensure lived on, even if it meant extinguishing hers.

One evening, alone in my office, I felt a moment of weakness. The image of Leah's face, her defiance and strength, haunted me, a whisper of what could have been. But I silenced the doubt. There was no room for weakness in this family, no room for softness. I had made my choice, and I would see it through.

The night Leah went into labour, I was ready, my heart hardened, my resolve unwavering. The doctor would follow through, and Ranger would never know. The family would survive, and one day I would have an heir moulded in my image, someone who would carry on the legacy I had fought so hard to build.

I knew this choice would come at a cost. But in a world ruled by power and strength, this was the only path forward. I would sacrifice Leah's softness for the family's survival. It was the way things had to be.

As I waited in silence, the decision finally settled in my heart like a stone, heavy and unbreakable. The future was secure, and nothing would stand in its way.

Chapter 3

In the weeks that followed, tension rippled through the family like cracks spreading across glass. Ranger had become more distant; his attention split between our world and Leah. I couldn't blame him, not entirely. She was his wife now, and it was natural that he'd want to be with her, especially as her due date approached. But his split focus was starting to show in the way he handled business, and, slowly, I could feel the walls closing in around us.

Rival families, scenting weakness, began making moves, subtle at first—an intercepted shipment here, a missing lieutenant there. But it was escalating. Word reached me of minor skirmishes on our territories, rival thugs testing our defences, pushing the limits of how far they could go. They were aware that Ranger wasn't closely monitoring the street-level operations, and they anticipated that these minor skirmishes would eventually escalate into a threat to everything we had established.

Ranger and I had always moved as one; he'd been like a shadow, silent and deadly, always there when I needed him. But lately, whenever I looked to him, he was with Leah or caught up in his own thoughts. I saw the way he softened around her, his face shedding years, his anger tempered by some deep, new contentment. Part of me understood it, even admired it. But admiration wasn't what kept the family alive.

One night, after another ambush left two of our men dead, I had enough. The rival families were exerting undue pressure, challenging the boundaries of my convened a meeting, inviting everyone to the estate and emphasizing that non-attendance would result in consequences for their disobedience. Ranger arrived late, apologising in hushed tones as he took a seat next to me. I nodded, but my silence was deliberate and pointed. He seemed to notice, his jaw tightening, but he held back his own response.

I addressed the room, my voice sharp and unyielding. "It's become clear to me that our family's strength is being questioned. Others think we've gone soft and that we're vulnerable. And why wouldn't they? We've lost men to pointless ambushes, and no one has answered for it." My gaze moved across each face, pausing briefly on Ranger. "It's time we remind them who we are. Fear is what keeps us at the top. Without it, we're nothing but prey for the scavengers."

The room nodded in agreement, the men's faces grim and resolute. Ranger, however, was watching me with a look of unease.

"What do you suggest, Silas?" He asked quietly, though there was an edge in his voice.

"We hit them back. Hard. I want every rival crew that's crossed us in the last month wiped out. Let them pick up their dead and remember why they feared us." I kept my gaze steady on him, waiting to see his reaction.

Ranger shifted, glancing at the men around us; the weight of the silence was almost palpable. "And what about the innocent people caught in the crossfire? These men have families too, Silas."

I resisted the urge to scoff, his words igniting a cold fire in my chest. "This isn't about them. They chose to go against us, and this is the price they pay. You're too soft, Ranger. You've forgotten what it takes to keep the family on top."

A shadow flickered over his face. "We can maintain our power without crossing every line, Silas. There's no reason to bring that kind of bloodshed to our door."

"Bloodshed is what keeps us safe!" I shot back, my voice rising. "You think our rivals care about our so-called morals? No. They'll take any weakness and exploit any crack in our armor. If we don't act now, if we let them think they can push us without consequences, then we might as well hand over everything we've built."

Ranger fell silent, his jaw clenched, but his eyes held a defiant edge that wasn't there before. Leah's influence was shifting something in him, something that had once been as solid as steel. I knew he cared about her, maybe more deeply than he'd ever admit, but that kind of love only made men weak in the end. I learned that lesson a long time ago.

The next night, I made sure that the message was sent clearly. We struck every group that had dared cross us, our retaliation swift and ruthless. The streets were left red with the blood of our enemies, bodies scattered as a brutal reminder of what it meant to defy us. I watched it all unfold from afar, the cold satisfaction settling over me like armour. Order would be restored, and our family's dominance would be indisputable.

Still, Ranger was different afterward. He didn't say anything outright, but I could see it in the way he avoided my gaze, the way he held himself stiffly whenever we were in the same room. It was a chasm that had never existed between us before, and it gnawed at me. He was drifting, caught in some moral dilemma that had no place in our world. The cracks were growing, and I could feel the edges of isolation beginning to close around me—the bitter realization settling in that perhaps I was the only one left who truly understood what it took to hold everything together.

One evening, I caught him alone, staring out over the garden where Leah liked to spend her afternoons. The glow of the city lights cast a shadow on his face, making him look older and weighed down.

"Do you have something to say, Ranger?" I asked, my voice quiet but steely.

He didn't look at me, his gaze fixed on some distant point in the darkness. "It doesn't have to be like this, Silas. You're pushing too hard. There's a balance we can find."

I felt a surge of irritation, the urge to shake him to make him understand the stakes. "Balance?" I repeated the word bitter on my tongue. "This isn't some game, Ranger. There is no balance here, only power. We either have it or we lose it. That's the reality."

He turned to me then, his eyes tired but determined. "Maybe that's your reality, Silas. But Leah, this family... they mean something beyond power. They give me purpose, a reason to do what I do. I don't want to lose that because we're too busy chasing fear and dominance."

For a moment, I couldn't even respond. The words felt like a betrayal, a knife twisting in my side. This was the man who had once been as ruthless as me, who'd understood what it took to survive in this world. Now, he was talking about purpose and balance, as if those things could keep the wolves at bay.

"You're losing sight of what matters," I said, my voice icy. "If you let your guard down, if you let Leah make you weak, this family will crumble."

He stepped back, the look in his eyes colder than I'd ever seen it. "Maybe it's not the family that's crumbling, Silas. Maybe it's just you."

The silence that followed was thick and heavy, the finality of his words settling like lead in my chest. For the first time, I felt a chasm open up between us, an irreparable fracture that neither of us could ignore. Ranger was slipping away, drawn toward a life I could never understand, a life that had no place in the world we had built. And with every step he took away from me, I felt more and more alone, isolated in a way that no power, no bloodshed, could ever fill.

That night, as I sat alone in the empty office, I realised that no one truly understood the weight I carried. They looked to me for strength and guidance, but they didn't see the cost. They didn't know the sacrifices, the ruthless choices I had to make to keep them all safe and to keep the family intact. Even Ranger, the one person I thought I could rely on, had been pulled away by softer things, leaving me to bear the burden alone.

The attacks from the rival families died down after our brutal retaliation, but the silence that followed was unnerving. It felt like a calm before a storm, a momentary respite that only served to highlight the fractures within our own ranks. Ranger was still by my side, still carrying out his duties, but the tension between us was undeniable, a constant reminder of the distance that had grown between us.

I found myself thinking about my father and about the choices he'd made to secure our family's future. He'd been ruthless and unyielding, and while I'd once resented him for it, I was starting to understand. Leadership demanded sacrifices, demanded a certain coldness that others couldn't comprehend. I'd inherited that mantle, taken on the same weight he had carried, but now, looking around at the family I had built, I felt the emptiness that came with it.

One night, as I walked through the darkened halls of the estate, I heard Leah's laughter echo from one of the rooms. She was with Ranger, their voices soft and warm, filled with a joy I hadn't heard in years. It was a foreign sound, one that felt out of place in our world of violence and bloodshed. And as I stood there, listening to the life they were building together, a life that had no room for the ruthless decisions I'd made, I felt a pang of something I couldn't name—a hollow ache that reminded me just how isolated I had become.

Ranger and Leah were creating a future that had no place for me, a future that clashed with everything I'd built. And as much as I wanted to protect them, to keep them safe within the walls of our family, I knew that our paths were diverging and that the choices I had made were carving out a loneliness that no amount of power could ever fill. The family was secure, its strength unquestionable, but as I stood there, alone in the shadows, I realised that I had paid a price that even I hadn't anticipated.

For the first time in years, I felt the weight of my own isolation, the knowledge that, in the end, the iron fist I had wielded had left me with nothing but empty echoes and a legacy built on blood. And there, in the darkness, I understood that power, while unbreakable, was also a prison, one that would keep me locked in its grip long after the last enemy had fallen.

Chapter 4

The longer I watched, the more it became evident that Leah was no ordinary addition to the family. She wasn't some peripheral figure, merely sitting in the background of our operation—she had woven herself into the fabric of our lives, slowly, quietly, and with a finesse that even I had to acknowledge was masterful. Leah was perceptive, more so than I'd initially given her credit for, and her presence was beginning to change things in ways I couldn't ignore.

Ranger had always been my rock, my trustworthy, loyal friend. But now... he was listening to Leah more and to me less. Her perspective, her empathy, seemed to seep into his decision-making, eroding the unwavering loyalty that had once been directed solely toward the family's cause. Ranger, my shadow, my second-in-command, was starting to openly question the ruthless methods we had always relied upon, and it was Leah's influence—I could see it, feel it. This was a situation I couldn't tolerate.

In the quiet moments, when I was alone with my thoughts, I would recall the stories of my father's rule, the tales of cold, relentless power that he wielded to keep this family in line. I had always known that this life demanded sacrifices and absolutes—a certain kind of coldness—to survive. My father's legacy had come at a cost, one I'd begrudgingly accepted when I took up his mantle. And now, I was starting to see a future where that legacy might be softened, tainted by the growing presence of Leah's influence over Ranger.

Leah's pregnancy had added a new dimension to this problem. Ranger was now caught up in thoughts of fatherhood, of providing a "better future" for his child, a future that didn't include the sacrifices we'd been forced to make to keep this family strong. The conversations I overheard, the subtle changes in his tone and in his eyes, told me that Leah's vision for their child didn't align with the iron rule I'd maintained all these years.

I could feel the distance growing between Ranger and me, widening with every whispered conversation and every tender glance he shared with her. He was shifting, changing, and Leah was the catalyst. I couldn't allow it, not when the family's legacy—its very survival—was at stake.

In my mind, there was only one solution. Leah had to be removed, and if I didn't act soon, this vision of softness and compassion she was nurturing in Ranger would spread, poisoning the family's core values. I thought about Ambrose, still just a child growing inside her. He was the future, my heir, but he needed to be shaped by the harsh truths of our world, not coddled by his mother's soft affections.

The decision weighed on me heavily. Despite my anger, there was a sliver of guilt gnawing at me, a whisper in the back of my mind that questioned if this was truly necessary. But every time that doubt surfaced, I forced it back down, convinced myself that I was doing what was best for the family and that this was the only way to preserve the legacy my father had built.

One evening, as the house lay shrouded in silence, I sat alone in my study, my thoughts consumed by the plan forming in my mind. I'd have to speak to the doctor, the one who'd attended to Leah throughout her pregnancy. He was a man who understood loyalty and knew what was at stake. A quiet conversation and a few subtle instructions would ensure the outcome. Leah's death would be tragic, yes, but it would be seen as an unfortunate consequence of childbirth. No one would question it, least of all Ranger, who would be devastated, left with only Ambrose to remind him of the life he'd envisioned.

The more I thought about it, the more certain I became. This wasn't just about removing Leah; it was about securing a future where my influence would remain intact, where Ambrose would grow up under the same relentless principles that had kept our family strong. I couldn't leave the family to a generation softened by sentiment and compassion.

The arrangement was nearly effortless. The doctor, an old friend of my father's, understood the need for discretion. When I broached the subject, his expression didn't even flicker. He listened in silence, nodded once, and assured me he'd handle everything. It was a relief, in a way, to have someone who understood the stakes, someone who wasn't tainted by Leah's influence.

A few days later, I observed Ranger with her, watching the way he doted on her, the warmth in his eyes that had once been reserved for our shared cause. There was something unsettling about seeing him like that, so different from the man I'd known. He had become vulnerable, softened by this domestic life he was building with her. I wanted to shake him, to remind him of the painful truths that had shaped us both, but I knew it would be pointless. Leah had her claws in him, and nothing I could say would change that.

The night before everything was set to take place, I found myself standing in the hallway outside their room, listening to the quiet murmur of their voices. They were laughing, a sound that felt foreign and out of place within these walls. It made my resolve falter, if only for a moment. But then I reminded myself of the bigger picture—of the sacrifices required to preserve what we had built. The laughter faded, replaced by a sense of grim determination. Tomorrow, everything would change.

The next morning, I was in my study when I received word that Leah had gone into labour. The doctor was already with her, as planned, and Ranger was by her side, his face a mixture of anxiety and anticipation. He barely noticed me as I entered the room, his attention wholly focused on Leah, who was breathing heavily, her face pale but resolute.

I watched them for a moment, my gaze drifting between Ranger's tense expression and Leah's weary but determined face. It was almost surreal, seeing her in that vulnerable state, knowing what was about to happen. I could sense the anticipation in the room, the weight of the moment pressing down on all of us.

Ranger glanced up, his eyes meeting mine for a brief second, and in that instant, I saw something that unsettled me—a glimpse of the old Ranger, the one who would have laid down his life for this family without hesitation. But it was gone as quickly as it had appeared, replaced by the softness that Leah had nurtured in him.

I left the room, retreating to the hallway where I waited; the minutes stretched on as the muffled sounds of Leah's labor filtered through the closed door. I couldn't bear to stay inside and watch the inevitable unfold, but I needed to be close enough to know the moment it happened. My hands clenched into fists, my mind racing as I reminded myself of the necessity of it all—of the future I was securing for Ambrose, for the family.

Then, suddenly, the silence was broken by a frantic shout. I couldn't make out the words, but I recognized the panic in Ranger's voice—the fear lacing his tone. A moment later, the door flew open, and the doctor stepped into the hallway, his face grim as he approached me.

"It's done," he murmured, his voice barely above a whisper.

I felt a wave of relief wash over me, mingling with a strange, hollow ache I couldn't quite identify. It was over. Leah was gone, and Ambrose would be raised without the influence that had threatened to weaken him, to soften his resolve. Ranger would grieve, of course, but in time, he would return to the family, his loyalty restored, unclouded by the distractions that had come with Leah's presence.

However, as I watched the doctor walk away, the weight of what I'd done settled heavily on my shoulders, a reminder of the sacrifices this life demanded. I had made the difficult choice, the one no one else could have made. It was my duty and my responsibility to ensure the family's survival, and I had done what needed to be done.

Ranger emerged from the room moments later, his face pale and his eyes hollow as he cradled the newborn in his arms. He looked at me, his gaze vacant and shattered, and in that moment, I felt a pang of something I couldn't name—a flicker of regret, perhaps, or a sliver of doubt.

However, it was already too late to take that action. The decision had been made, the future secured. All that remained was the legacy I had fought to preserve—a legacy that would carry on through Ambrose and be shaped by the same principles that had kept our family strong. And as I looked into Ranger's broken eyes, I reminded myself that this was the cost of power, the price we paid to ensure the survival of what we had built.

In the end, it was all that mattered.

Chapter 5

The day Leah went into labor, a strange, heavy silence had settled over the house. It was an oppressive silence, thickening the air like storm clouds before the first crack of thunder. Every corner seemed to anticipate the outcome that would unfold, though only I knew the real gravity of the situation. Leah's labor marked the beginning of the final step in securing the family's future—a future I'd fought and sacrificed for, one that would now be fortified and free from any disruptive influence.

Leah had unwittingly become a threat, one that I could not afford to let grow any stronger. Ranger's loyalty, his resolve, and even his clarity had started to fracture under her influence. I'd watched him soften; I watched him question the decisions I knew were necessary to preserve our power. Leah had brought compassion to a world where it had no place, and I knew it would only spread if she stayed. Ranger, once my unwavering right hand, was beginning to think with his heart instead of his head.

By morning, I received word that Leah's labor had started. I called the doctor who had worked for me forever to execute my plan. He was a man I trusted implicitly, a man who understood the value of loyalty in our world and the consequences of betrayal. I had briefed him a week prior, laying out every detail with calculated precision. As most would, he was initially hesitant, but my words forced him to agree. He had assured me, finally, that he understood what was required.

As I entered the room, Leah was breathing heavily, her face pale and slick with sweat. Ranger was by her side, clutching her hand, his eyes glued to her face in silent, fervent support. His attention was so focused that he barely noticed me. His expression was unguarded, brimming with a raw vulnerability that stirred something deep within me—a weakness I couldn't allow him to indulge. This was the moment where everything would change for both of them, and he had no inkling of what was truly at stake.

I moved to the corner, watching the scene unfold with a calm, impassive gaze. Leah's laboured breaths filled the room, mingling with the quiet murmurs of the doctors and nurses who bustled around her. Ranger kept his hand on her shoulder, whispering reassurances I could barely hear. For a moment, an irrational impulse clawed at me, urging me to turn away and reconsider. However, the memories of every sacrifice I had made, every hard choice I'd endured to keep this family at the top, rose up to quell that thought. This was necessary, a calculated step to ensure that our legacy continued unchallenged.

Time passed slowly, and I waited, hands clasped behind my back, listening to the ebb and flow of strained voices and the anxious rustle of medical equipment. It felt as though hours had passed before I saw the doctor exchange a look with me. It was time.

I watched as he leaned down toward Leah, speaking in a voice meant for only her and Ranger to hear, though I caught every word. He explained, in a tone laced with feigned concern, that complications had arisen and that the baby's life was in jeopardy. He told them that in situations like this, the mother and child were sometimes forced to choose. Leah's eyes widened, her gaze flickering to Ranger, who gripped her hand tightly, his face white with shock.

The weight of the doctor's words sank in slowly, dragging them down into a suffocating silence. Ranger's face was a mask of disbelief, an expression that twisted painfully as he tried to grasp what was being asked of him. Leah reached out, squeezing his hand, her expression filled with a calm acceptance that surprised me. She nodded slowly, meeting Ranger's gaze, and in that moment, it was as though they had reached some silent understanding.

I felt a strange satisfaction settle over me as I watched the exchange. Ranger would believe he had no choice—that this was an unavoidable tragedy rather than the calculated maneuver it truly was. He would mourn, he would grieve, but he would ultimately come to terms with it as a tragic loss rather than an act of betrayal. And Ambrose would be left to carry on our legacy, unshackled by the softness Leah might have instilled in him.

The doctor made his way over to me, his expression grim, though I could see the steely resolve in his eyes. "It's done," he murmured, barely above a whisper. I nodded, offering him a brief acknowledgement before he turned back to his task. Ranger and Leah remained locked in their silent communion, unaware of the part I had played in orchestrating this outcome.

The minutes that followed were marked by the sounds of muted activity and the quiet, tense atmosphere of a medical emergency unfolding. I watched as the doctor administered the necessary treatment, his hands moving with practiced efficiency, ensuring that Leah's fate was sealed while maintaining the illusion of a genuine effort. Ranger's attention remained fixed on Leah, his face a mix of desperation and helplessness, oblivious to the truth.

As Leah's breaths grew shallow, a quiet realization seemed to settle over her—her eyes flickering between Ranger and the doctor, perhaps sensing the inevitability of what was happening. She gripped Ranger's hand tightly, her voice barely a whisper as she spoke to him, her words too soft for me to catch. Whatever she said seemed to provide him with a measure of comfort, a last connection before the final curtain fell.

The moment of her passing was marked by a sudden stillness, a quiet finality that filled the room. Ranger's face crumpled, his shoulders sagging as he pulled Leah's lifeless hand to his chest, his expression one of utter devastation. He held her close, his grip fierce and unyielding, as though refusing to let go, even in death.

The weight of the moment pressed down on me, an odd sense of detachment mingling with an unsettling emptiness. Leah was gone, her influence removed, and with it, the threat she posed to our family's future. Ambrose would be raised under my guidance, without the interference of softness or sentimentality. I had secured the legacy, achieved the goal that had driven me for so long. And yet, watching Ranger's grief, I couldn't ignore the hollow ache that gnawed at the edges of my resolve.

As the room emptied, I approached Ranger, placing a steadying hand on his shoulder. He flinched at my touch but didn't look up, his gaze fixed on Leah's still form, his grief radiating from him like a palpable force. I offered him a few quiet words of condolence, though they felt hollow even to my own ears. He nodded mutely, barely acknowledging me, and I left him to his mourning, stepping out into the hallway, where the silence felt suffocating.

In the solitude of the corridor, I allowed myself a moment to process what had transpired. Leah was gone, and with her, any threat to the family's stability. Ambrose would grow up with the strength and ruthlessness necessary to lead, unburdened by the softness that might have clouded his future. The family's legacy was secure, preserved in its unyielding form, free from the influence that might have weakened it.

As I made my way back to my study, the weight of my actions lingered—a constant presence that pressed down on me, even as I tried to brush it aside. Power cost us in order to preserve what we had built. I reminded myself of the necessity and of the greater good that would come from this sacrifice. Ranger would grieve, yes, but he would come to understand, in time, that this was the only path forward. Ambrose would grow into the role we needed him to fulfil, shaped by the principles that had kept our family strong.

That evening, as I sat alone in my study, the silence felt heavier than ever. I poured myself a glass of whisky, the amber liquid catching the dim light as I contemplated the events that had unfolded. Leah's face lingered in my mind, her final moments replaying in vivid detail, and I found myself wrestling with a strange sense of unease.

I had done what was necessary. I had ensured the survival of our legacy and taken the steps required to secure the future. Yet, as I sat there, nursing my drink in the dim light, I couldn't shake the gnawing emptiness that had settled deep within me—an ache that went beyond simple regret or guilt. I suppose it reminded us of the price of life and the sacrifices we made for power and loyalty.

In the days that followed, I watched as Ranger struggled to come to terms with his loss, his grief a constant presence that cast a shadow over everything he did. He threw himself into his duties with a fervour that bordered on desperation, as though he were trying to drown his sorrow in the work that had once been his refuge. I saw the toll it took on him—the way his face grew haggard, his eyes hollow and haunted. And though I knew he would eventually find a way to move forward, I couldn't help but feel a pang of something I couldn't quite name.

In my pursuit of power, in my unwavering determination to preserve the family's legacy, I had sacrificed more than I cared to admit. Leah's death had secured the future, yes, but it had also left an indelible mark on all of us, a scar that would linger even as we moved forward. And as I looked toward the future, I couldn't shake the feeling that, in securing the family's strength, I had lost something I could never reclaim.

Chapter 6

The days following Leah's death cast a heavy shadow over the family. Every corner of the house seemed to carry the weight of her absence, a quiet emptiness that was almost oppressive. Ranger moved through it like a ghost, his usually sharp gaze dulled, his shoulders carrying an invisible burden. I watched him closely, taking in his grief, the depth of which I had both anticipated and quietly dismissed. Yet, the impact of it—the way it seemed to consume him entirely—was an unforeseen complication. I had expected him to mourn, yes, but I hadn't considered how profoundly her death would alter him.

Ranger's loyalty, however fractured it appeared, was still intact. That much, at least, I could count on. But it was a loyalty now tainted with sorrow—a sorrow that seemed to take root in the very foundations of his being. And as the days turned into weeks, the weight of his grief only intensified, permeating his every action, casting a shadow over every decision he made.

He spoke less, moved with a distracted lethargy, and often drifted into his own thoughts, lost in memories of Leah. I found myself studying him, trying to gauge how deeply her loss had altered his convictions. Our conversations were brief, marked by an awkward distance that hadn't existed before. And as he grieved, I shifted my focus elsewhere. It was time to look to the future, to mold the family's next heir in a way that would ensure our legacy continued, untainted by the softness Leah had represented.

Ambrose, now only days old, was a blank slate, untouched by the world and its harsh realities. He was everything I needed—a pure, unformed potential, one that I would shape from the beginning, free of interference. His future was in my hands, and I would ensure that he grew into the man our family required: decisive, ruthless, unyielding. The path I had laid out for him was a narrow one, forged from the same iron principles that had kept us at the top.

Ranger, however, had other plans. He lingered over the infant, his rough, calloused hands cradling Ambrose as though the child were something fragile, something precious. His face softened in those moments, his eyes losing their haunted, hollow look. I watched from a distance, noting the way he held the child, the way he looked at him, as though Ambrose was the only thing keeping him grounded. It was a weakness, a vulnerability I could not afford him to indulge.

I remained distant, detached, allowing Ranger his moments with Ambrose while I quietly solidified my plans. The boy would be raised under my guidance, molded in a way that would ensure he grew to embody the values that had sustained us. Ranger's influence, however subtle, would be curtailed. His loyalty was still intact, yes, but his grief had created a fissure between us, one that widened with every passing day. He was distracted, caught in the web of his own sorrow, and it was a distraction that I would not tolerate.

As the weeks turned into months, Ranger's grief began to manifest in ways that were both troubling and irritating. He questioned my decisions more frequently, his tone laced with a quiet defiance that hadn't been there before. It was subtle, almost imperceptible, but it was there—a quiet resistance that simmered beneath the surface. His grief had changed him, making him less pliable and less willing to follow without question.

One evening, as we sat across from each other in the study, I noticed the shift in his gaze, a hardening that hadn't been there before. He looked at me, his eyes sharper, more focused, as though he were searching for something beneath the surface. I met his gaze evenly, my expression unreadable, but I could feel the tension building between us, a tension that had only grown since Leah's death.

"Silas," he began, his voice steady and controlled. "Have you ever questioned the cost of all this?" He gestured vaguely, his hand encompassing the room, the house, and the life we'd built. There was a hint of something in his tone—a note of accusation, veiled but unmistakable.

I kept my expression neutral, refusing to let him see any hint of reaction. "The cost is irrelevant," I replied, my voice cold, detached. "We do what is necessary to preserve the family. Sentiment has no place in this life, Ranger. You know that as well as I do."

He looked away, his jaw tightening, a flicker of frustration passing over his face. He had expected a different answer—perhaps some acknowledgement of the sacrifices we'd made and the blood we'd pilled. But I had nothing to offer him—no comfort, no reassurance. My focus was on Ambrose, on the future I was building, and Ranger's grief was an obstacle, a distraction I could not afford to indulge in.

Yet, even as I distanced myself from Ranger, as I poured my attention into shaping Ambrose's future, a quiet unease settled over me, a nagging sense that Ranger's grief was more than just sorrow. There was a bitterness there, a slow-burning resentment that festered beneath the surface, and though he remained loyal, I could feel the subtle shift in his demeanour. It was a seed of discontent, planted deep, one that I knew could grow into something dangerous if left unchecked.

I hardened myself against it, focusing instead on Ambrose and the task at hand. Ranger's grief was his own burden to bear, his own weakness to confront. I had given him Leah's memory and allowed him his moments of mourning, but that was all I could afford him. The future required a different kind of strength, a resolve that would not be swayed by sentiment or sorrow.

Ambrose was a quick learner, sharp, and observant even at his young age. I watched him closely, noting the way his eyes followed every movement, every sound, and his gaze filled with a quiet intensity that reminded me of myself. He was a child, yes, but there was potential there—a raw, unformed strength that I could shape and mold into the weapon our family needed. I began his training early, instilling in him the principles that had guided me and the lessons I had learned through blood and sacrifice.

Ranger, however, seemed to resist my influence, his presence a constant reminder of Leah's lingering legacy. He was protective of Ambrose, overly attentive, and though he remained respectful, there was a quiet tension between us, an unspoken conflict that simmered beneath the surface. He questioned my methods and my decisions, his tone laced with a quiet defiance that grated against my patience.

One night, as I watched Ranger cradle Ambrose, his gaze softened by an emotion I could not name, a flicker of something dark stirred within me. Leah's influence lingered, a ghostly presence that haunted our every interaction, and I knew that her memory would continue to shape Ranger's actions and his decisions. He was tethered to her still, bound by a loyalty that had not died with her, and it was a loyalty that threatened to undermine everything I had worked to build.

I tightened my grip on Ambrose's future, distancing myself further from Ranger, solidifying my plans with ruthless efficiency. The family's survival depended on strength, on an unyielding resolve, and I could not afford to let sentiment cloud our path. Ranger's grief was a weakness, a vulnerability that could be exploited by our enemies, and though he remained loyal, I could feel the cracks beginning to form, subtle but undeniable.

In the quiet of the night, as I sat alone in my study, I contemplated the future, the legacy I had fought to preserve. Ranger's presence loomed in the background, a constant reminder of the sacrifices I had made and the lives I had taken to ensure our survival. His grief was a weight that hung over us, a shadow that darkened every corner of our world, and though he remained loyal, I knew that his loyalty was fragile, a brittle bond that could shatter under the strain of our shared history.

Ambrose's future was secure, his path laid out before him, free from the softness that had threatened to weaken our family. Yet, as I watched Ranger's grief deepen, his sorrow morphing into a quiet, simmering anger, I could not shake the feeling that the price of our survival was higher than I had anticipated. The legacy I had fought to preserve was a heavy burden, one that grew heavier with every passing day, and though I had secured our future, I could not ignore the shadow that lingered, a reminder of the cost of power, the sacrifices we had made, and the fragile bond that held us together.

In the end, it was a balance, a delicate equilibrium that teetered on the edge of collapse, a legacy built on blood and sacrifice, held together by the thin thread of loyalty, and as I looked toward the future, I knew that the weight of our past would continue to haunt us, a shadow that could never be fully banished, a reminder of the price we had paid for power.

Chapter 7

The days following Leah's death hung over us like a dense fog, and grief's weight had settled heavily over the Farill family. The loss affected each of us differently, but mourning in this life of ours meant keeping one eye always open. Rivals could sense vulnerability with a predator's precision, and Leah's death had indeed left us exposed. It didn't take long for the wolves to close in; their first moves probed our defenses for weaknesses.

They struck at our people in the dead of night, sending a clear message: they believed the Farills had softened. Silas Farill's once-iron hold was now, in their eyes, a grip weakened by sentiment. Perhaps they thought that Ranger, consumed by his grief, would falter or that I'd lost my own edge. But they would learn just how wrong they were.

The attacks were precise and coordinated—strikes on our supply lines, ambushes on our men in known locations—even our allies were caught off guard. It was as if they'd been watching for weeks, gathering information on our movements and exploiting every possible vulnerability. I had underestimated the depth of their planning, a mistake I would not make again. Ranger had lost his wife, and I'd lost someone who represented a future I hadn't entirely understood but now saw was a liability. Their assumption that this would cripple us was their first mistake.

"Silas," Ranger spoke, his voice a low growl as he stood in the dim light of my office. His grief was still raw, a visible scar that somehow made him even more dangerous. There was a new ruthlessness to him. His usual calm, his tendency toward restraint, had vanished, replaced by a relentless thirst for retribution. "They don't know what they've started."

There was something almost foreign in his voice—a hardness that was new, cutting, vicious. For a brief moment, I wondered if this was an ally or a man twisted beyond recognition by grief. Yet, even in his changing demeanor, I saw potential. Ranger's willingness to embrace violence was a new weapon in our arsenal, one I was prepared to wield without hesitation.

I let silence settle between us before responding. "Then let's show them," I said, leaning forward, my tone steady and calculated. "The family will not be seen as weak. We retaliate. No mercy, no hesitation."

Ranger nodded, his face a mask of fury tempered by purpose. Previously, he was the strategist, always anticipating three moves ahead, but now, he acted with a sense of finality that I had never witnessed before. Leah's death had broken something in him— fractured the very foundation of who he was—and I could see the fragments of his former self fading into something darker, something merciless. It was a change I recognized well; it was the same transformation that had shaped me years ago.

Our first response was swift and brutal. We hit back hard, striking at our enemies' strongholds, leaving a trail of bodies as a message. Every move was calculated, a carefully orchestrated display of power that would send shockwaves through the underworld. Our rivals thought they had the upper hand, but I was determined to remind them who held the real power.

As the dust settled from each strike, I observed Ranger with a critical eye. There was no hesitation in his actions, no restraint. He moved with an efficiency that was both impressive and unsettling. It was as if Leah's death had stripped away whatever humanity he had left, leaving only a cold, ruthless machine.

However, even as I trusted him more with each strike, a sliver of doubt lingered in the back of my mind. His grief-fueled fury was now an asset, but grief was unpredictable and volatile. It could drive a man to unthinkable lengths and twist his motives in ways even he wouldn't recognize. For now, he was focused and committed to our cause, but how long would that last? How deep did his loyalty run?

As our assault escalated, Ranger began to show an intensity that bordered on obsession. He was relentless, pushing himself and our men to the brink, driven by a need for vengeance that was almost palpable. It was as if he was trying to bury his grief in blood, each killing a temporary balm for the wound Leah's death had left. I admired his tenacity and his dedication, but I couldn't shake the feeling that his loyalty was becoming something fragile, a thread that could snap under the wrong pressure.

One night, after a particularly brutal attack, I found myself alone in my office, the weight of our actions settling heavily on me. The darkness around me seemed to mirror the darkness I felt within, a creeping paranoia that I couldn't ignore. I trusted Ranger, yes, but trust in this world was a luxury, one that often came at a steep price. I had built this family on a foundation of ruthless pragmatism, and if Ranger's loyalty wavered, I wouldn't hesitate to act.

The next morning, as I watched Ranger interact with Ambrose, I felt a surge of unease. His affection for the child was genuine, a bond that was as strong as any blood tie. But it was a bond that could be manipulated or exploited. I couldn't afford any weakness, not when our enemies were circling, waiting for any sign of vulnerability. I would closely monitor Ranger's love for Ambrose, as it was both a strength and a liability.

The retaliation continued, each strike more brutal than the last. We left a trail of bodies, each one a message to our enemies that the Farill family was not to be trifled with. Ranger spearheaded the assault, his ferocity wielding a blade-like power that sliced through our adversaries. But even as he became more ruthless and more efficient, I could see the cracks beginning to form.

One evening, as we prepared for yet another assault, Ranger turned to me, his gaze hard, unyielding. "This is what you wanted, isn't it?" he asked, his tone laced with a quiet accusation. "To remind them of our power?"

I met his gaze, my expression unreadable. "This is what is necessary," I replied, my voice cold, detached. "Power is the only language they understand. We show weakness, and they'll tear us apart."

Ranger looked away, his jaw clenched, a flicker of something unreadable in his eyes. For a brief moment, I wondered if he saw through my facade, if he knew that his newfound ruthlessness was exactly what I needed—a tool to ensure our survival. But if he did, he said nothing, his silence a tacit agreement to continue our bloody campaign.

The tension between us grew, a quiet animosity that simmered beneath the surface. We moved through our roles, orchestrating each attack with a cold efficiency, but the unspoken conflict remained, a constant reminder of the rift that Leah's death had created. I could see the toll it was taking on Ranger—the way his grief had transformed him into something unrecognizable, a man driven by a need for vengeance that bordered on self-destruction.

Yet, even as I relied on his ruthlessness and trusted him to lead our men into battle, I couldn't shake the feeling that his loyalty was slipping and that his grief was slowly eroding the foundation of our alliance. He was a man on a precarious path, his loyalty vulnerable to the crushing weight of his sorrow. I had seen it happen before— see men driven to madness by loss, their grief twisting their motives until they became unrecognizable.

I kept a close watch on him, my paranoia growing with each passing day. He was still loyal, yes, but how long would that last? How deep did his loyalty truly run? As I observed him, I saw the subtle changes and the quiet defiance that simmered beneath his surface. He was no longer the man I had known, the man who had once been content to follow my lead without question.

One night, after another successful strike, I found myself alone with Ranger in the quiet of my study. The silence between us was heavy, filled with unspoken tension. I could see the toll the violence had taken on him—the way it had hardened him, turned him into something cold and unfeeling. But there was something else there, a darkness that I couldn't ignore.

"We've sent a message," he said, his voice low, almost weary. "But at what cost?"

I met his gaze, my expression unreadable. "The cost is irrelevant," I replied, my tone cold, detached. "We do what is necessary to survive."

Ranger looked away, his jaw clenched, a flicker of something unreadable in his eyes. For a brief moment, I wondered if he saw through my facade, if he knew that his newfound ruthlessness was exactly what I needed—a tool to ensure our survival. But if he did, he said nothing, his silence a tacit agreement to continue our bloody campaign.

As I watched him leave, a quiet sense of unease settled over me. The bond between us was weakening, the foundation of our alliance eroding under the weight of his grief and my paranoia. He was still loyal, yes, but for how long? How much longer would he follow me? Would he accept my decisions without question?

In the end, I knew that trust in this world was a fragile thing, a bond that could be broken with a single act of betrayal. And as I watched Ranger disappear into the shadows, I couldn't shake the feeling that our alliance was built on borrowed time, that the loyalty we shared was a brittle thread that could snap under the weight of our shared history.

The rivals would come again, no doubt emboldened by what they perceived as cracks in our family. But they'd find no mercy, no hesitation. The Farill family remained formidable, and my leadership would guarantee the continuation of our legacy. However, I was aware that Ranger's loyalty was a distinct issue.

Chapter 8

The echoes of our past decisions linger, and I know Ambrose senses them even if he doesn't yet understand them. It has been two years since Leah's death, and although he is still young, he is sharp, already absorbing everything like a sponge. Ambrose is, in many ways, a mirror of the boy I once was—full of potential but with an innocence that must eventually be shed. This legacy demands it. And so, the time has come to begin his training, a process I know all too well but one that I feel strangely hesitant to enforce.

In the still mornings when I first bring him to the training grounds, I catch myself searching his face, as if looking for a remnant of Leah's softness. I know it's there, hidden in his wide-eyed curiosity, his fascination with the world. There's a light in him, a spark of something pure, and yet, if he is to carry this family's name, that purity must be extinguished, replaced by steel and resolve. I am his father, but I must also be his teacher, his guide into the life he was born to inherit.

Ranger's role in Ambrose's life has complicated things in ways I hadn't anticipated. Since Leah's death, Ranger has spent more time with Ambrose than I have, teaching him small things—basic skills, discipline, survival. He's become a fixture in Ambrose's world, an influence I cannot overlook, and I see how much Ambrose adores him. Their bond, however, gnaws at me. The trust between them, the effortless affection... it is a bond I can't replicate, nor one I feel I should have to. Ambrose is my son, my blood, and yet he looks at Ranger with an admiration that I find both enviable and infuriating.

One day, as we're working through a lesson in hand-to-hand combat, Ambrose struggles with the sequence of moves. He's young, of course, and the skill will come with time, but frustration flashes in his eyes. I recognise it—it's the same frustration that used to grip me as a boy—the fear of failing, of being less than what's expected. I place a hand on his shoulder, steadying him, but the instinct to demand perfection runs deep. He senses it, too, his gaze lifting to mine, a question hovering there.

"What if I'm not good enough?" His voice is barely audible, a fleeting moment of vulnerability that seems almost alien.

"You will be," I reply, my voice firm. "You're a Farill. And we don't give up. Not ever."

I can see my words resonate with him, and he straightens, determination hardening his small features. But there's a shadow in his eyes, a flicker of doubt that I know all too well. I've taught him strength, but have I also taught him fear? The realisation unsettles me.

Over the next few months, Ambrose grows more confident, his movements sharper, more controlled. He absorbs every lesson I give him—every tactic and every strategy—as if he were born for it. But despite his progress, he still turns to Ranger with a reverence that stings. Ranger, with his quiet encouragement and subtle guidance, has become the steady presence that Ambrose relies on, and it's a role I feel slipping from my own grasp.

One evening, I find them in the courtyard, Ranger showing Ambrose how to handle a knife, his movements precise and measured. Ambrose watches him with wide eyes, mimicking each movement, his focus absolute. Ranger smiles at him, a rare softness in his expression, and I feel a surge of resentment rise within me. Ranger is not Ambrose's father. That role belongs to me, but here they are, forming a bond that feels closer than any I've managed to forge with my own son.

As I approach, Ranger looks up, his gaze meeting mine with a calm confidence that only deepens my irritation. He's aware of the tension between us, I can tell, but he masks it well, hiding any hint of rivalry behind a facade of loyalty. Ambrose notices me too, his face lighting up with a smile that is both genuine and tentative, as if he's uncertain of my approval.

"Father, look what Ranger taught me," he says, holding up the knife with a hint of pride. He demonstrates the grip Ranger showed him, his hands steady, his posture poised. For a moment, I am both proud and resentful, torn between acknowledging his skill and despising the fact that it's Ranger's guidance he values most.

"You've done well, Ambrose," I say, keeping my voice steady. "But remember, it's not just about skill. It's about control. A steady hand is nothing without a sharp mind."

Ambrose nods, his expression serious, and I feel a pang of guilt for the harshness in my tone. But this is the path he must walk, the lessons he must learn. There is no room for softness, no room for weakness. And yet, in moments like these, I wonder if I am truly preparing him for the life he must lead or simply projecting my own fears and insecurities onto him.

Ranger senses the tension between us, his gaze flicking between Ambrose and me with a subtle wariness. He's careful not to overstep, but I can see the protectiveness in his eyes, the silent defiance that lurks beneath his calm exterior. He knows that he has become a father figure to Ambrose, and he's aware of how it affects me. But rather than distance himself, he seems to embrace the role, as if daring me to confront him.

"Ambrose is a quick learner," Ranger says, his voice even, his expression neutral. "He has a natural talent. Reminds me of someone else I once knew."

There's an unspoken challenge in his words, a reminder that he knows my past, my struggles, better than anyone else. For years, Ranger has been my confidant, my right hand, the one man I could rely on without question. But now, with Leah's influence lingering in his life, with Ambrose looking to him for guidance, our bond has become fraught, tainted by a rivalry that neither of us fully acknowledges but both feel acutely.

Days pass, and I throw myself into Ambrose's training with renewed intensity. Each lesson becomes a test, a challenge to push him further and to mould him into the leader I know he can be. He's young, but he learns quickly, his resilience a testament to the legacy he's inherited. But as I watch him grow, I can't help but feel a pang of regret, a creeping doubt that gnaws at the edges of my resolve.

I remember my own training, the lessons Carlo drilled into me with ruthless efficiency, the constant demand for perfection. There was no room for softness, no space for vulnerability. Every mistake was punished, every weakness exposed, and though it made me strong, it also left scars that have never fully healed. And now, as I see the same resolve harden in Ambrose's eyes, I wonder if I am condemning him to the same fate, if I am shaping him into a man who will one day look back on his childhood with resentment.

One evening, as Ambrose practices his marksmanship, I find myself standing beside him, watching as he lines up each shot with meticulous precision. There's a cold determination in his gaze, a focus that is both impressive and unsettling. He's barely ten years old, and yet he carries himself with the weight of a man twice his age.

"You're doing well," I say, breaking the silence. "But remember, this isn't just about hitting a target. It's about discipline and control. Every shot must be deliberate, every decision calculated."

Ambrose nods, his expression serious, and for a brief moment, I see a flicker of uncertainty in his eyes. It's a look I recognize all too well—a reminder of the boy he once was, the child who still clings to some semblance of innocence. But it's a look that fades quickly, replaced by a steely resolve that both comforts and disturbs me.

As he lines up his next shot, Ranger appears, his presence a silent challenge. He watches Ambrose with a proud smile, a warmth in his gaze that I can't replicate. Ambrose glances at him, a hint of admiration in his eyes, and I feel a surge of jealousy, a bitterness that I struggle to contain.

"You're doing well, Ambrose," Ranger says, his voice filled with a quiet pride. "Your father taught you well."

The words are meant as a compliment, but they feel like an accusation, a reminder that Ranger has become a constant presence in Ambrose's life, a man who has taken on a role that should be mine. I force a smile, nodding in acknowledgement, but the resentment lingers, a simmering tension that I can't shake.

Over the next few weeks, I watch as Ranger's influence over Ambrose grows, his presence a constant reminder of the bond they share. I see the way Ambrose looks to him for guidance, the admiration in his eyes, and I feel a pang of jealousy that I can't ignore. Ranger has become more than just a mentor; he has become a father figure, a man who embodies the qualities that Ambrose values most.

And yet, despite my resentment, I can't bring myself to confront Ranger and challenge the bond they share. I know that Ambrose needs guidance, that he needs a man he can look up to, a role model who embodies the strength and resilience that our legacy demands. But as I watch them together, I can't shake the feeling that

I am losing something precious, that I am being slowly edged out of my own son's life.

In quiet moments, I find myself grappling with a sense of loss, a feeling of isolation that I can't explain. I have built this family, forged a legacy that will endure long after I am gone, and yet, as I watch Ranger and Ambrose together, I feel a growing sense of emptiness, a hollow ache that I can't ignore.

Perhaps it is the curse of this life—the price we pay for power and control. We are men shaped by violence, hardened by loss, and yet, in moments like these, I wonder if we are truly strong or simply broken. Ambrose is my son, my blood, and yet, as I watch him with Ranger, I can't shake the feeling that he is slipping away from me, that the bond we share is being slowly eroded by a man who has become both my ally and my rival.

And so, as I continue to train Ambrose to mold him into the leader he must become, I am haunted by a single, unshakeable truth: that one day he will look back on this life, on the lessons I have taught him, and he will see not a father but a man who shaped him through fear and control, a man who sacrificed everything for a legacy that may ultimately cost us both everything.

Chapter 9

Every move we've made has been calculated and precise, but in recent months, the Farill family has turned ruthless. Under our leadership, we've systematically crushed each rival family that dared challenge us. One by one, their empires have crumbled, leaving a trail of blood and ashes in our wake. We've set a new standard, one that speaks of dominance and an unwavering resolve to remain on top. But as we ascend, my attention sharpens on the details, the small shifts that whisper something's out of place.

As I review our latest operations reports, I notice a disturbing trend. In recent months, certain decisions have been made without my explicit approval. Men have been moved, alliances shifted, and strikes ordered without my signature or even my input. I've never questioned Ranger's loyalty before—he's been my shadow, my closest ally. But there's a growing sense of unease, a suspicion that his motives may be shifting. My eyes narrow on his name, stamped beside decisions that were once mine alone to make.

At first, I let it pass. Ranger has consistently demonstrated decisiveness and action, and I am confident that he acts in the family's best interest. But now I wonder if his actions aren't motivated by something else, something personal. As time passes, he seems to be testing his family influence and establishing his own territory. I can't shake the feeling that he's positioning himself as something more than my right hand.

One evening, after a particularly brutal strike on one of our last rival clans, Ranger and I sit across from each other in my office, surrounded by the weight of our actions. He's calm, his expression a mask of control, but there's something new in his gaze, a glint of independence that I can't ignore. I bring up the recent decisions, my tone carefully controlled.

"You've been making moves without consulting me, Ranger," I say, watching his reaction closely. "We're a team. Decisions like these should come through me."

Ranger's expression barely shifts, though I catch the slightest flicker of something behind his eyes—something that makes my suspicions coil tighter.

"Silas," he says, his voice steady. "These are actions we both knew needed to be taken. I thought it best to act swiftly. There's been enough talking, enough waiting. The family needs to see strength."

Strength. The word echoes, and I sense a hidden meaning in it. I've built this family on strength, but I am its leader, its final authority. Ranger's actions feel like a quiet rebellion, a test to see just how far he can go.

"Strength," I repeat slowly, letting the word sink in. "You think I'm not showing strength?"

"No, it's not that." He shakes his head, but the answer feels rehearsed, evasive. "It's that we're facing pressures like never before. Enemies are watching, waiting for any sign of weakness."

I scrutinize him, my expression hardening. Although I understand the logic in his words, his actions have gone too far. "Remember your place, Ranger," I say, my voice low and deliberate. "This family thrives because we move as one. We act as one."

For a moment, his gaze meets mine—a subtle challenge there, a hint that he's not as bound to our hierarchy as he once was. He nods, though, his expression neutral. "Of course, Silas. I've never forgotten."

The conversation ends, but the tension remains—an invisible wall between us. I can feel the strain in every encounter—the unspoken power struggle that has begun to surface. Ranger's respect for me was once unshakeable, but now something has changed. I see it in the way he holds himself, the way he speaks to others, and the way he makes decisions that echo my own, as if he's laying a claim on the family's future.

Days pass, and Ranger's influence only seems to grow. The men respect him; some even look to him with the same loyalty they show me. I sense their admiration, their quiet trust in him, and it gnaws at me, a reminder that power is as much perception as it is action. I built this family and forged it with blood and sacrifice, but Ranger is becoming more than just an ally. He's becoming a figurehead in his own right, a man with enough charisma to sway the loyalty of those closest to us.

One night, after Ambrose has gone to bed, I sit alone in my office, the dim light casting shadows across the room. I pour myself a drink, letting the burn of the whisky settle my nerves, but the unease remains, gnawing at me. I run through Ranger's recent actions in my mind, dissecting each decision and deviation from my orders. It's as though he's testing his own reach, seeing how much he can influence without my approval.

I realise, then, that Ranger is positioning himself in a way that feels all too familiar. He's seen how power is wielded and how decisions shape loyalty, and he's using that knowledge to his advantage. But why? The question lingers, a whisper of doubt that grows louder with each passing day. Is he planning to challenge me, to take what I have built and make it his own?

The thought chills me. I know Ranger, or at least I thought I did. We've fought together, bled together, and I trusted him with more than just my life. But power changes people; I've seen it happen before. And as much as I want to believe he would never betray me, I can't ignore the signs.

The family meetings become more tense, our conversations laced with an undercurrent of rivalry. Ranger speaks with authority, his words measured but commanding, and I can see the men hanging on his every word. They respect him, perhaps even admire him, and it infuriates me. I am their leader, the one who made them what they are, but Ranger's presence has shifted something—a quiet rebellion that stirs beneath the surface.

One evening, after a particularly heated meeting, I confront him alone. The room is empty, the others having filtered out, leaving us in a charged silence. I don't hold back; my voice edged with anger.

"You're overstepping," I say, my tone sharp. "You're making decisions as if you're the one in charge."

Ranger's gaze meets mine, unflinching, and for a moment, I see something in his eyes that I can't quite decipher. "Someone has to make these decisions," he replies, his voice calm but firm. "We can't afford to hesitate, not now."

"Hesitation?" I scoff, my anger flaring. "I built this family on decisiveness. You're acting as though you have a claim to something that isn't yours."

Ranger's jaw tightens, and there's a flash of defiance in his eyes, a spark that only fuels my suspicion. "I'm doing what needs to be done, Silas. For the family. For Ambrose."

Ambrose. The mention of my son's name feels like a slap, a reminder that Ranger has positioned himself not only as my right hand but as a father figure to Ambrose. It's a role he's assumed without my permission, and the realisation hits me like a punch to the gut. He's not just challenging my authority; he's laying the groundwork for his own legacy, his own claim on the family's future.

I take a step closer, my voice dropping to a low, dangerous tone. "You may think you're doing what's best, but don't forget who put you where you are. Don't forget whose name built this empire."

For a moment, Ranger holds my gaze, his expression unreadable. But then he nods, a faint smirk playing at the corner of his mouth, as though he's indulging me, as though he knows something I don't. It's a look that unsettles me, a reminder that power, once given, is not easily taken back.

"Of course, Silas," he says, his tone respectful but with an edge that I can't ignore. "I've never forgotten."

However, as he walks away, I know that his words mean little. Ranger has not forgotten; he's simply biding his time, testing his influence, waiting for the moment when he no longer has to answer to anyone.

The days that follow are marked by an uneasy silence, a cold distance that settles between us. I watch him carefully, noting every interaction and every decision, searching for signs of betrayal. And as the family continues to grow to expand its power, I feel the weight of my own mistrust bearing down on me, a paranoia that I can't shake.

Ranger has become a force within the family, a man whose influence rivals my own, and though he plays his role with careful precision, I know that he is positioning himself for something more. He may not have made his move yet, but I can see it in his eyes, in the way he commands the loyalty of our men, in the way he speaks with an authority that no longer defers to mine.

As I lay awake at night, my mind racing with thoughts of betrayal, I realized that the time had come to make a choice. I have two options: either I continue to observe Ranger and allow him to establish his own authority within the family, or I take action and remind him of the hierarchy that has maintained our strength. But I know that either path comes with a price, a cost that will only deepen the rift between us.

In the darkness, I wrestle with my decision, the weight of it pressing down on me. I have built this family and forged its legacy, but now, as I face the prospect of betrayal from within, I wonder if the true threat to our empire is not from our enemies but from the man who once stood by my side.

Only time will reveal the depths of Ranger's loyalty, but as I lie there, staring into the shadows, I know one thing with chilling certainty: the moment of reckoning is coming, and when it does, only one of us will emerge victorious.

Chapter 10

The silence between us has grown sharper, cutting through every interaction, every exchange, with a biting tension. Ranger's actions continue to drift from mine, an independence that grates against my authority. Each time he moves without consulting me, each time he takes command without my nod of approval, my patience thins. Today, after weeks of watching his every move, I can't hold back any longer. I call him into my office, the place where our plans were first forged, where loyalty was once cemented between us.

Ranger arrives promptly, his expression guarded, yet he doesn't look away. His stance, his gaze—they're steady, but they lack the deference that was once so deeply ingrained. There's something different about him—a quiet challenge, a sense of resolve that only adds to my suspicions. I gesture for him to sit, though neither of us makes a move toward the chairs.

"Ranger," I say, my voice calm but cold. "You've been making decisions without consulting me. I think you know that's not how things work here."

He crosses his arms, his stance unfazed. "With all due respect, Silas, I thought you'd appreciate initiative. Isn't that what you've taught us? To act swiftly, decisively?"

"Swiftly," I echo, my gaze narrowing, "but not independently. There's a difference, Ranger. A difference you seem to have forgotten."

His jaw clenches, and I catch a glint of something hard in his eyes. "The family's growing, Silas. The more we expand, the more decisions need to be made on the fly. I'm only doing what's necessary."

"Necessary?" I can barely contain the edge in my voice. "Since when did you decide what's necessary? I built this family from the ground up. Every decision is mine, and I expect loyalty."

"I am loyal," he says, though there's a tension in his voice that tells me he's holding something back. His hands, clenched into fists, betray his frustration. "I've always been loyal. But I'm not going to sit by and let us become vulnerable because you think every move has to be yours."

A cold anger pulses through me. "Watch your tone."

He pauses, as though weighing his words, then finally nods. "I'm sorry, Silas. I meant no disrespect."

However, the apology feels empty and perfunctory. A line has been crossed, and he knows it as well as I do. For a moment, we stand there in silence, the air thick with unspoken tension. I search his face for any sign of weakness, any hint of betrayal, but he holds my gaze steadily, unflinching. This is no longer the Ranger I once knew, the man who followed my orders without question. This is someone else, someone with his own ambitions, his own agenda.

The confrontation ends, but the suspicions remain. I know now that Ranger is slipping beyond my control and that his loyalty is no longer as absolute as it once was. He's become a man of his own making, and that makes him dangerous. I've seen ambition like his before—the kind that leads men to make decisions without regard for loyalty or allegiance. And as much as I want to believe he's still on my side, I can't ignore the signs any longer.

Days pass, and my thoughts turn darker. The seeds of doubt, once small, have taken root, spreading through my mind until they're impossible to ignore. Every decision Ranger makes, every order he gives without my approval, feels like a challenge, a direct threat to my authority. He's testing his own power, seeing how far he can push the boundaries, and I know where this path leads. I've seen it before in men who once claimed loyalty but turned their backs when it suited them.

And then the memory of Leah surfaces—the way she looked at Ranger, the way she softened him, the way her influence began to shift the dynamic between us. I recall the decision I made—the cold calculation that led to her death. It was a choice driven by necessity, by a need to secure the future of this family. And now, as I watch Ranger's influence grow, I know I may have to make that same choice again.

It's not easy, this knowledge, this understanding of what must be done. Ranger has been with me since the beginning; we've shared battles, victories, and losses. But the family comes first, always, and if he's forgotten that, then he's no longer my ally. He's my enemy.

I begin to lay out my plans carefully, cautiously. Every move must be calculated; every detail must be accounted for. I cannot afford mistakes, not now. This time, there must be no witnesses and no unresolved issues. Ranger must be eliminated in such a way that it appears natural and inevitable. I reach out to a few trusted men, those whose loyalty I can still count on, and lay the groundwork for what must come.

Each step I take is deliberate and precise, mirroring the same ruthlessness I once showed Leah. I instruct my men to monitor Ranger's movements, to track his meetings, his decisions. Slowly, the pieces begin to fall into place, a plan taking shape that will ensure my control over the family remains unchallenged.

One evening, as I sit alone in my office, I consider the weight of my decisions and the cost of this path I've chosen. This sense of isolation, hovering between loyalty and betrayal, is a familiar feeling. Ranger was once my closest ally, the man I trusted above all others. But trust is a fragile thing, easily broken, and in our world, loyalty must be proven again and again.

A knock at the door interrupts my thoughts, and I look up to see Ranger standing there, his expression unreadable. He steps inside, closing the door behind him, and I can feel the tension between us—a taut, unspoken conflict that hangs in the air.

"We need to talk," he says, his voice steady but with an edge that tells me he's not here for pleasantries.

I gesture for him to sit, though I remain standing, my gaze fixed on him. "What is it?"

"There's been talk," he begins, his tone cautious. "Some of the men... they're concerned about your decisions, about the direction the family's heading."

"Is that so?" I ask, my voice carefully neutral. "And what do you think, Ranger?"

He hesitates, his gaze flickering briefly, and I can see the conflict in his eyes. "I think we're growing and expanding, and sometimes your... approach doesn't allow for the kind of flexibility we need."

"Flexibility," I repeat, letting the word linger in the air. "You mean independence."

His silence is answer enough, and I feel the final thread of trust snap. He is no longer concealing his intentions or acting as a loyal subordinate. He wants more, more control, more influence, and he's willing to challenge me for it.

"I understand, Ranger," I say, my tone cold and dismissive. "Perhaps you should remember who put you where you are."

He stands, his expression hardening, and I see a flash of defiance in his eyes. "With all due respect, Silas, the family's future is bigger than either of us."

For a brief moment, two men engaged in a silent struggle for dominance. I can see it in his eyes—the ambition, the hunger for power that mirrors my own. He's become a rival, a threat, and I know that he must be dealt with, just as I dealt with Leah.

As he leaves, I feel the finality of the decision settle over me, a cold certainty that Ranger's time is drawing to an end. There can be no room for hesitation, no room for mercy. I cannot afford weakness, not now, not ever.

Over the next few days, I put the finishing touches on my plan, each step designed to ensure Ranger's fate is sealed. I instruct my men to isolate him, to make it look like an accident, a mishap that no one could have predicted. The irony is not lost on me—that once again, I am forced to destroy someone close to me in the name of loyalty.

As the plan unfolds, I feel a strange sense of detachment, as though I'm watching it all from a distance. The weight of my decisions, the cost of this life I've chosen, bears down on me, yet I push forward, knowing that this is the only way. Ranger may have once been my closest ally, but loyalty in this world is a fleeting thing, a luxury I can no longer afford.

On the night it is to happen, I sit alone, waiting for the call, the confirmation that Ranger's fate has been sealed. The minutes tick by slowly, each one a reminder of the path I've chosen and the sacrifices I've made to keep the family strong. And when the call finally comes, a quiet voice on the other end telling me it's done, I feel a strange emptiness, a hollowness that lingers long after the line goes silent.

I've secured my control and eliminated the last threat to my authority. But as I sit there, alone in the darkness, I can't shake the feeling that something vital has been lost, that in my quest for power, I've sacrificed more than just those who stood in my way.

And as the night wears on, a haunting realisation settles over me—a sense that perhaps the true cost of loyalty is something I can never regain.

Chapter 11

The truth came to Ranger like a silent storm, building slowly, bit by bit, until the full weight of it threatened to crush him. At first, it was just a lingering question, a quiet suspicion he dismissed as paranoia. But over time, hints surfaced—subtle, unremarkable fragments of conversations, whispers that he overheard but hadn't wanted to process. And now, standing here, his mind racing as the pieces fell into place, Ranger felt the nauseating reality of it. Silas had orchestrated Leah's death, coldly, calculatingly, to secure his control over the family and Ambrose.

The thought alone was enough to bring Ranger to his knees.

For a moment, he let himself feel it all: the deep ache, the wave of grief for Leah that he thought he had buried, the raw rage that bubbled up, uncontainable, and the growing sense of betrayal that carved him open. He clenched his fists, his breath catching in his chest as he struggled to remain composed. But the weight of it was unbearable. Not only had Silas, his mentor and the man who had once been like a father to him, taken Leah's life, but he had also stolen his family's future for his own control.

Ranger's jaw clenched, and his hands shook as he pressed them to the rough surface of the desk in front of him, feeling the cool solidity under his fingers. The room around him faded, and all he could see, all he could feel, was the memory of Leah: her laughter, her gentle smile, the warmth that filled any space she occupied. And Silas had extinguished it without a second thought, turning her death into a necessary evil, just another step in his climb to power.

He forced himself to take a breath, steadying the rage that boiled beneath his calm exterior. Leah had once told him that vengeance was a poison and that it would only consume him if he let it. But now, her words felt like a distant memory, a whisper that had long been silenced. There was no peace left to hold onto, no love to soothe the turmoil within him. Silas had seen to that.

It wasn't long before Ranger's despair crystallized into something sharper and more defined—a purpose. Silas would pay. But he wouldn't confront him outright—no, not yet. This betrayal called for more than just anger; it called for carefully orchestrated revenge, a retribution that would mirror the calculated cruelty Silas had inflicted. If Silas wanted control, he would get it, but Ranger would ensure that it would come at a cost he couldn't bear.

The first step was to control his emotions and mask the hatred that now colored every thought and every interaction he had with Silas. For weeks, Ranger forced himself to wear a calm facade, a mask of loyalty that betrayed nothing of the fire raging inside him.

He continued to attend family meetings to fulfill his duties, all the while observing Silas with quiet, smoldering resentment. Silas, oblivious to the truth Ranger now held, continued as if nothing had changed. His confidence was infuriating, a reminder of the cruelty he wielded so effortlessly.

Ranger's mind, sharp and calculating, began to shift focus away from grief and into strategy. He needed allies, men who would stand by him without question when the time came. It wouldn't be easy—Silas's influence was deeply entrenched, his control absolute. But Ranger knew the family well—he knew the men who had served under them for years. He suspected some of them harbored their own grievances against Silas, even if they were too afraid to voice them. Silas's rule was unchallenged, but that didn't mean it was uncontested.

In the months that followed, Ranger built his alliances carefully, choosing his confidants with precision. He avoided the men who were bound to Silas through blood or undying loyalty, instead focusing on those who had felt the sting of his ruthless decisions. He engaged them in discreet discussions, gently suggesting and hinting that the family's course could alter if a sufficient number of them expressed a desire for change. It was a slow, delicate process, but gradually he sensed the shift. The loyalty that had once been Silas's strength was beginning to fracture, replaced by a simmering resentment that Ranger could now use to his advantage.

Every night, when he was alone, Ranger would allow himself to remember Leah and feel the loss that never truly faded. He pictured her as she'd been—vibrant, compassionate, unafraid to speak her mind. She had seen the darkness within the family but had believed that it could be tempered, that love and loyalty could soften its edges. Ranger had shared her vision once and had believed in it with everything he had. But now, her death had shattered that ideal, and he understood that the family's legacy would never change. It was built on blood and betrayal, and he had to accept that to survive.

The day of reckoning came unexpectedly—a sudden opportunity that Ranger recognized immediately. Silas had arranged a gathering, a show of strength for the family and its allies. It was the kind of display Silas thrived on, a reminder of his authority and his unchallenged dominance over everyone in the room. The Ranger could see it in the way Silas held himself—the subtle arrogance that had begun to creep into his demeanor over the years. Silas was certain of his power and his control—so much so that he failed to notice the cracks forming in the foundation he'd built.

As the night wore on, Ranger bid his time, waiting for the perfect moment to strike. He watched Silas, noting every gesture, every word, and the way he held court over the room with a confidence that bordered on complacency. And then, when the evening was at its peak, Ranger finally made his move.

He approached Silas with a calm expression; his demeanor was controlled, giving no hint of the storm raging inside him. "Silas, a word?" he said, his voice steady.

Silas looked at him, a faint flicker of irritation crossing his face before he nodded, following Ranger to a quieter corner of the room. "What is it?" he asked, his tone dismissive.

For a moment, Ranger said nothing, simply studying the man before him. This was the man who had once been his mentor, his friend, the man who had guided him into this world. And yet, standing here now, Ranger saw only a stranger, a man who had sacrificed everything in his pursuit of power, including the people who had once been closest to him.

"Do you ever regret it, Silas?" Ranger asked quietly. "The choices you've made, the people you've sacrificed?"

Silas's eyes narrowed, a hint of suspicion in his gaze. "What are you talking about?"

Ranger forced himself to keep his expression neutral, his tone casual. "Leah. She wasn't just my wife, Silas. She was part of this family. Did her life mean anything to you?"

Silas's expression hardened, his gaze sharpening. "Leah knew the risks. She understood what it meant to be part of this family."

The words struck Ranger like a blow, a brutal confirmation of the truth he already knew. Silas hadn't cared, not truly. He had used Leah as a pawn in his game, discarding it when it was no longer useful.

Something inside Ranger snapped, a final break in the fragile restraint he'd maintained for so long. He felt his control slip, the mask he'd worn for months beginning to crumble. But he forced himself to remain calm, to keep the fury at bay.

"I see," he said quietly. "Then you won't mind if I take a more active role in ensuring the family's future."

Silas's gaze sharpened, a flicker of unease crossing his face. "Be careful, Ranger warned. "You're walking a fine line."

Ranger smiled, a cold, bitter smile that held none of the warmth it once had. "So are you, Silas. And I suggest you remember that."

With those words, he turned and walked away, leaving Silas standing alone, his expression unreadable. The confrontation had been brief, but it had been enough. Ranger had made his intentions clear and had drawn the line in the sand. And now, there was no turning back.

In the days that followed, Ranger's plan began to take shape. He moved carefully and deliberately, consolidating his alliances and securing his influence within the family. The men who had once been loyal to Silas were beginning to shift their allegiance, drawn to Ranger's quiet authority and his calm resolve. Silas, for all his power, had become a relic of the past, a symbol of an era that was fading. And Ranger was ready to step into the void to claim the power that had once been Silas's alone.

However, he knew that this was only the beginning and that the real battle was yet to come. Silas would not go down without a fight, and Ranger was prepared for the struggle that lay ahead. He would not rest until justice was served, until Silas paid the price for Leah's death. And when the time came, Ranger would be ready.

The memory of Leah guided him, a constant reminder of the debt he owed, the vengeance he had sworn to exact. Silas had taken everything from him and had destroyed the life he had once cherished. But now, Ranger would take it all back, piece by piece, until there was nothing left of Silas's legacy but ashes.

And when the final reckoning came, Ranger would stand over Silas's broken empire, a testament to the power of loyalty, of love, and of the unbreakable bond that even death could not sever.

Chapter 12

Ambrose was growing fast, and with every day, Silas felt the slow erosion of his grip over the family. It was subtle at first—the small moments when Ambrose would listen to Ranger more closely than to his own father, or the way he followed Ranger's instructions without question. Silas noticed how, over the years, the young boy had begun looking at Ranger the way he used to look at him—with a respect that ran deeper than admiration. It was unsettling to see how that bond had deepened over time, becoming stronger and more formidable than Silas had anticipated.

It seemed that every lesson he tried to instill in Ambrose was subtly challenged, diluted by Ranger's influence. In meetings, Ambrose's young eyes would drift toward Ranger, following his movements and listening to his every word, seemingly unaffected by Silas's presence. It was a strange experience for Silas to feel as though he were slowly being sidelined in his own family, yet he couldn't shake the feeling that this was, perhaps, the fate he had long set in motion.

Silas had always understood that Ambrose would one day need a strong figure to mold him and guide him through the dark parts of the world he was born into. But he had never imagined that the boy would begin to see Ranger as that figure. Ranger, who had once stood by his side as a trusted ally, was beginning to hold a different sort of power—a quiet, undeniable influence over Ambrose. And it became harder to ignore with each passing day.

Silas remembered the relationship he'd once had with his own father, the suffocating control that had pushed him to his limits. It was what had driven him to act ruthlessly, to carve his own path through the brutal lessons he had been taught. He had told himself he would never repeat those mistakes and that Ambrose would grow into his role with guidance, not coercion. But now, watching Ambrose's loyalty lean toward Ranger, Silas couldn't help but see the echo of his father's iron grip—and the consequences that had come with it.

Ranger had not openly defied Silas in front of Ambrose, but there were moments when the boy would bring up something Ranger had said that contradicted his own teachings. The message was always delivered carefully, yet the intent was unmistakable. Ranger's influence was evident, and the subtle challenges felt like small stones cast into an already turbulent pond.

Silas felt the tension rise within the family, not as an open conflict but as a slow, creeping shift in the power dynamics. Ranger's presence grew more assertive, his decisions more autonomous, and his words more carefully woven with authority. It was clear that he was positioning himself as a leader within the family, though not by any direct declaration. He seemed to understand that leadership could be taken with subtler actions, by guiding Ambrose's choices and influencing the men around him without ever needing to declare his intentions aloud.

One evening, as they gathered around the long, polished table for dinner, Silas watched the interplay between Ranger and Ambrose more closely than ever. Ambrose's gaze was fixed on Ranger, his young face showing admiration and interest. Ranger, sensing the attention, spoke to him in a tone that Silas couldn't ignore—warm, familiar, like a father passing down wisdom to his son. Silas grated his teeth, forcing himself to hold back his thoughts as he watched them exchange words. The others around the table seemed to sense the underlying tension, their eyes flicking from one to the other, but no one dared to break the silence.

Afterward, Silas found himself alone in his office, staring at the dark city skyline, wondering when things had started to slip out of his hands. The room felt colder than usual, and he could hear the faint hum of life beyond the walls, the sound of a city that had once seemed unattainable. But now, standing there, he felt strangely detached from it all. The family he had spent years building, the power he had sacrificed so much for—he could feel it slipping through his fingers like sand.

In the days that followed, Ranger's position within the family seemed to grow stronger still. The men who had once looked to Silas for every decision now glanced at Ranger, waiting for his nod, his approval. The respect Silas had once commanded was shifting, not in a way that was obvious to anyone who hadn't been paying close attention, but in a way that felt undeniable to Silas. He could sense that the loyalty of his men, once unshakeable, was now divided, split between him and the man who had once been his closest ally.

Silas attempted to dismiss it, convincing himself that Ranger was merely assuming the role he had always prepared him for. But deep down, he knew that it was something more, something darker, a quiet revenge that Ranger was enacting, not with words or accusations, but with loyalty and admiration slowly taken from him. Ranger had no need to confront him directly; he was dismantling Silas's authority from within, one small interaction at a time, and Silas was powerless to stop it.

As Ambrose grew older, his respect for Ranger became more apparent, and Silas felt the walls closing in around him. He saw in Ambrose's eyes the same look he had once given his own father— that mixture of reverence and defiance, the kind of loyalty that only half belonged to him. And each time he saw it, Silas felt the ghost of his past lurking closer, haunting him with the memory of choices he had once believed were justified.

One evening, Silas called Ambrose into his study, hoping to speak with him alone to reclaim some of the bond he felt slipping away. The boy entered the room with a confidence that was both impressive and unsettling, a self-assuredness that reminded Silas too much of his own youth. Ambrose was growing into a young man with a mind of his own, a strength that Silas recognised but didn't know how to contain.

They spoke for a while about small things, about the business and the responsibilities that Ambrose would one day shoulder. But as the conversation turned toward the family's future, Silas sensed an invisible wall between them, an understanding that Ambrose was holding back, measuring his words carefully. Silas's questions became more pointed, probing at the core of what was truly on his mind.

"Ambrose," he said, his tone serious, "there are lessons you'll need to learn if you're to lead this family one day. Hard lessons. I won't lie to you; it won't be easy."

Ambrose met his gaze, his young face set in a determined expression that was both a comfort and a warning. "I understand, Father. Ranger has been teaching me about the weight of those responsibilities."

Silas felt a flash of anger rise within him, though he kept it from his face. He wanted to shout to demand that Ambrose look to him and not to Ranger for guidance. But instead, he nodded, forcing himself to remain calm.

"Ranger has his ways," Silas replied, his voice quiet. "But remember, Ambrose, there's only one leader in this family. Only one man understands what it takes to carry that weight."

Ambrose said nothing, his eyes unreadable, and Silas felt the cold sting of doubt once more. His own words seemed hollow, lacking the conviction he had once felt. The boy nodded, but Silas knew that he hadn't truly heard him and that his loyalty was divided in a way that could not be undone.

In the following months, Ranger continued his subtle campaign, guiding Ambrose, shaping his values, and moulding him into the leader Silas had envisioned—but not under his control. Ranger's influence was undeniable, and Silas felt the weight of it with every decision and every quiet word spoken between them. He could see Ranger's revenge playing out in the most calculated way—a slow erosion of his power that left him feeling isolated and haunted by the mistakes of his past.

Silas had sacrificed so much to protect his family's legacy, to ensure that his son would rise to take his place. But now, as he watched Ambrose's loyalty shift toward Ranger, he realised that he was losing everything he had fought to hold. Everything he had once held dear, including control, influence, and even his family, was gradually disappearing, leaving him with nothing but the hollow shell of a legacy that no longer belonged to him.

He was haunted by the choices he had made—the ruthless decisions he had believed were necessary to secure his power. The shadows of his past loomed over him—a constant reminder of the price he had paid—and he could feel the cycle repeating itself, this time with Ambrose and Ranger at its center.

Silas pondered over the possibility of regaining what he had lost, bringing Ambrose back to his side, and reminding him of the loyalty that was rightfully his. But no matter how he tried, he could not bridge the divide that had formed, a gap widened by the silent, calculating revenge that Ranger had set in motion.

And in the end, Silas was left with the bitter realisation that he had become his own worst fear—a man who had lost control, who had sacrificed everything only to watch it slip away. The legacy he had built was crumbling, and there was no one left to blame but himself.

Chapter 13

Silas knew the confrontation was coming long before Ranger stepped into the room. Ranger's recent observation of him revealed a fire in his eyes, a simmering fury that had been patiently waiting for its opportunity. Silas had tried to avoid this moment, to maintain a semblance of control over the family and his own tenuous grip on Ambrose. But it seemed that time was up.

Ranger entered the room in silence, closing the door firmly behind him. Silas sat at his desk, his back straight, hands clasped before him as he watched Ranger cross the room with a deliberate calm that was more unsettling than rage. Ranger's face was unreadable, his eyes fixed on Silas with an intensity that cut through the silence, a blade of judgement honed over years of unspoken resentment.

"Silas," Ranger began, his voice low and steady. There was no hint of affection in it, no trace of the loyalty that had once bound them together. "We need to talk."

Silas met his gaze, holding his composure even as he felt the weight of Ranger's words. "I've been expecting this," he replied, his voice as controlled as his expression. "You've never been one to let things lie."

Ranger's lips twisted into a bitter smile. "I suppose that's true. And I think it's time we stop pretending that everything between us is fine, that Leah's death was just... a tragedy of circumstance." He leaned forward, placing his hands on the desk between them, his gaze piercing. "I know what you did, Silas. I know you let her die."

The accusation hung in the air, heavy and undeniable. Silas held Ranger's gaze, feeling the enormity of the moment settle over him like a shroud. He had known this reckoning would come, but he had hoped it would be years from now, with enough distance and time to dull the truth.

"I did what I had to," Silas said, his voice even but carrying an undertone of steely resolve. "I made a decision for the good of the family, for Ambrose, for all of us."

Ranger's face twisted with rage, his hands clenching into fists on the desk. "For the family?" he echoed, his voice trembling with barely restrained fury. "You murdered Leah. You let her die to serve your own twisted need for control, to ensure Ambrose grew up without a mother's love. Don't hide behind 'the family,' Silas. This was about you."

Silas took a slow, measured breath, struggling to maintain his composure in the face of Ranger's wrath. "You think I wanted to hurt you, Ranger?" he said, his voice rising. "You think this was easy for me? I knew what it would mean and what it would cost. But I did it because someone had to. Leah's influence over you was... was changing you. She was softening you, making you weak. Ambrose needed a strong example to follow, not a life of sentiment and indulgence."

Ranger's jaw tightened, his hands trembling with the force of his rage. "You talk about strength, Silas, but you're the weakest man I've ever known," he spat, his words laced with venom. "You let your own fears control you; let them drive you to kill the woman I loved. The mother of your own grandchild. All for what? So you could keep your precious legacy safe? You've built nothing but a hollow empire, a family that's rotting from the inside because of your obsession with control."

Silas felt a surge of anger rise within him, a fierce indignation that he could no longer contain. "You think you understand what it takes to lead this family?" he demanded, his voice sharp. "You have no idea the sacrifices I've made or the blood I've shed. Everything I've done, I've done for the sake of this family. And if that means making hard decisions, then so be it."

Ranger's gaze hardened, his eyes like cold steel. "Sacrifices?" he repeated, his voice a deadly whisper. "The only sacrifice here was Leah's life. And you made it, Silas. Not for the family, not for Ambrose, but for yourself."

Silas felt his composure beginning to crack, the weight of Ranger's accusations bearing down on him with a force that was almost physical. He had spent years justifying his choices, telling himself that every decision he made was necessary and that every life he took was for the greater good. But now, faced with Ranger's unrelenting fury, he felt the hollow ring of those justifications echoing in his mind.

"Leah's death was a tragedy," he said, his voice wavering. "But it was a tragedy that needed to happen. She would have made Ambrose weak, Ranger. She would have softened him and turned him into a man who couldn't survive in this world. I did what I had to, and I would do it again if it meant protecting this family."

Ranger's face contorted with grief and rage, his fists clenched so tightly that his knuckles were white. "You murdered her," he said, his voice choked with emotion. "You killed the woman I loved, Silas. And you took away the mother Ambrose deserved, the one person who could have given him a chance at a life beyond this nightmare you've created."

The room fell into a tense silence, the air heavy with the weight of Ranger's words. Silas could feel the foundations of his world crumbling around him, the carefully constructed lies he had told himself beginning to unravel. For the first time, he was forced to confront the truth of his actions, to face the reality of the choices he had made.

Still, he could not allow himself to falter—not now, not after everything he had sacrificed. He straightened his shoulders, his voice hardening with resolve. "I did what was necessary," he said, his tone cold. "Leah's death was a price I was willing to pay for Ambrose's future. For the future of this family."

Ranger's eyes blazed with fury, his entire body radiating with a tension that threatened to explode at any moment. "You're a monster, Silas," he said, his voice trembling with barely contained rage. "And you're too blind to see it. You think you're saving this family, but all you're doing is destroying it from the inside out."

Silas felt his own anger flare in response, a fierce indignation that burnt through his veins. "And what would you do, Ranger?" he demanded, his voice rising. "Would you have let Leah live, let her coddle Ambrose until he was too weak to survive in this world? Would you have sacrificed everything we've built, just to spare your own feelings?"

Ranger's gaze hardened, his fists clenching at his sides. "I would have chosen love over fear, Silas. I would have given Ambrose a chance at a life beyond this endless cycle of blood and violence. But you... you chose to murder the one person who could have saved him from this fate."

The words cut through Silas like a knife, a raw, searing pain that he had never allowed himself to feel before. He had spent his life building walls around his heart, convincing himself that every choice he made was justified and that every life he took was a necessary sacrifice. But now, faced with the full weight of Ranger's grief and rage, he felt those walls begin to crumble—the cold, unyielding armor he had built around himself shattering into pieces.

Ranger took a step forward, his face inches from Silas's, his voice low and deadly. "You took everything from me, Silas," he said, his words laced with a cold fury that sent a chill down Silas's spine. "And now, I'm going to take everything from you."

Silas felt a surge of fear rise within him, a visceral, gut-wrenching terror that he had not felt in years. He had always believed himself to be untouchable, a man who could control every aspect of his life and every facet of his family. But now, faced with Ranger's unrelenting rage, he realised that he was not as invincible as he had once believed.

Ranger's fist shot out, connecting with Silas's jaw with a force that sent him staggering backward. The pain was sharp—a white-hot explosion that radiated through his skull—but he barely registered it, his mind reeling with the shock of the attack. He stumbled, his hand reaching out to steady himself against the edge of the desk, his vision blurred by the sudden onslaught of pain.

Ranger advanced on him, his face twisted with rage, his fists clenched in preparation for another blow. Silas felt a surge of panic, a desperate need to regain control, to reassert his authority over the man who had once been his closest ally. But Ranger was relentless, his movements swift and brutal, his fists connecting with Silas's body in a series of punishing blows that left him gasping for breath.

As he fought to defend himself, Silas felt the weight of his own choices bearing down on him—the realization that he had brought this upon himself. He had sacrificed everything for the sake of power, for the illusion of control, and now he was paying the price. The pain was relentless, a searing reminder of the consequences of his actions, and he knew that he could no longer escape the truth.

Finally, Ranger stepped back, his chest heaving with exertion, his face twisted with a mixture of rage and grief. Silas lay on the floor, his body bruised and battered, his vision swimming with pain. He struggled to sit up, his hand reaching out to steady himself against the edge of the desk, his breath coming in ragged gasps.

Ranger looked down at him, his expression cold and unyielding. "This is just the beginning, Silas," he said, his voice a low, menacing whisper. "I will make you pay for every life you've destroyed, every lie you've told, and every sacrifice you've forced upon this family. And when I'm done, there will be nothing left of the empire you've built."

Silas felt a chill run down his spine, a bone-deep fear that he had not felt in years. He had always believed himself to be untouchable, a man who could control every aspect of his life and every facet of his family. However, now, facing with Ranger's unrelenting rage, he realised that he was not as invincible as he had once believed.

As Ranger turned and walked away, leaving Silas broken and bloodied on the floor, he felt the full weight of his choices crashing down upon him, a brutal reminder of the price he had paid for power. And in that moment, he knew that he was truly alone—a man haunted by the ghosts of his own making, a king whose kingdom was crumbling from within.

Chapter 14

Silas stood in the darkened room, his pulse thrumming as he waited for Ranger to arrive. He had summoned him here, to the very heart of the Farill estate, the same place where their family's fortunes had once been forged and fractured. Silas had wanted to meet Ranger here, in a space soaked in history and secrets, where it all had begun. Every corner of the room was filled with memories that clung to him like ghosts, reminding him of the choices he had made—the lives he had ended, the family he had betrayed.

Ambrose stood nearby, watching them both with a wary, uncertain gaze. He was young, too young to truly understand the stakes of the confrontation unfolding before him, but there was a keen intelligence in his eyes that made Silas uneasy. Ambrose was a product of everything Silas had built, yet the boy remained a stranger to him. He was a mystery, an unfinished canvas onto which Silas had tried to paint his own legacy, but something in the boy resisted. Ranger, Silas thought bitterly, his jaw tightening. Ranger's influence had seeped into Ambrose, undermining the image Silas had sought to create.

Ranger finally entered the room, his expression hard, his shoulders set with a purpose that Silas recognized all too well. There was no hesitation in his movements, no uncertainty in his gaze. This was a man on a mission, a man who had been waiting for this moment. Silas could feel the unspoken words between them, the weight of years of resentment and betrayal pressing down on them both.

"So, here we are," Silas said, his voice low and steady, though his heart hammered in his chest. "The loyal lieutenant, finally standing up to the boss."

Ranger's mouth twisted in a bitter smile. "Loyalty? You wouldn't know the meaning of the word if it hit you in the face, Silas. You taught me what loyalty means—to the family, to the blood we've spilled. But you betrayed all of that the moment you chose power over those you claimed to protect."

Silas felt a surge of anger rise within him, his hands clenching at his sides. "I did what was necessary," he said, his voice laced with a steely resolve. "Every choice I made, every life I took, was for the family's sake. I built this empire from the ground up. Without me, there would be nothing left but dust and ashes."

Ranger took a step closer, his gaze hard, unyielding. "What you built, Silas, was a legacy of blood and betrayal. You've turned this family into something monstrous, something twisted. And now, it's time for that legacy to end."

The words struck Silas like a blow, a cold, hard truth that he had tried to avoid acknowledging for years. He had spent his life building walls around himself, convincing himself that his choices were justified, that every sacrifice he made was necessary. But now, faced with Ranger's unwavering gaze, he could feel those walls beginning to crumble.

Silas's voice shook with barely restrained rage. "And you think you can do better?" he demanded. "You think you can take everything I've built and make it something pure, something good? You're just as ruthless as I am, Ranger. You don't have the strength to lead this family."

Ranger's face was set, his eyes cold and unyielding. "Maybe I am ruthless," he said, his voice steady. "But at least I know where my loyalties lie. You killed Leah, Silas. You murdered the woman I loved, the mother of your own grandson, all for the sake of your own twisted ambition."

Silas felt a pang of guilt at Ranger's words, a small, gnawing doubt that he quickly crushed. Leah's death had been a necessary sacrifice, a calculated decision made for the sake of the family's future. He had convinced himself of this truth over and over again, repeating it like a mantra until he could no longer hear the whispers of doubt.

"Leah was a distraction," Silas said, his voice cold. "She would have softened you, made you weak. I did what needed to be done."

Ranger's fists clenched, his entire body trembling with rage. "You're a monster, Silas. And now, it's time for you to pay for everything you've done."

In that moment, Silas knew there would be no more words, no chance for reconciliation or understanding. They were beyond that now, beyond the bonds of loyalty and blood that had once bound them together. This was a fight to the death, a battle for control of the family, and Silas knew that only one of them would walk away from this room alive.

Ranger lunged at him, his fists swinging with a force that sent Silas staggering backward. Silas barely had time to raise his arms in defense before Ranger's blows rained down on him, each strike fueled by years of pent-up rage and resentment. The pain was sharp, a brutal reminder of Ranger's strength, and Silas struggled to hold his ground, his vision blurring with each impact.

However, Silas was no stranger to violence. He had spent a lifetime fighting, clawing his way to the top, and he was not about to let Ranger take everything he had built without a fight. With a snarl, he struck back, his fists connecting with Ranger's jaw, his ribs, each blow driven by his own desperation, his own fear of losing everything he had worked so hard to achieve.

The fight was brutal, a savage clash of wills that left both men battered and bloodied. They stumbled through the room, knocking over furniture, their breaths coming in ragged gasps as they struggled to overpower each other. Silas could feel his strength waning, the years of paranoia and guilt weighing him down, slowing his movements, but he forced himself to keep fighting, to push through the pain.

As they grappled, Silas caught sight of Ambrose standing in the doorway, his eyes wide with horror as he watched his father and grandfather tear each other apart. The sight of the boy sent a surge of anger through Silas, a renewed determination to end this fight and secure his legacy once and for all.

"Stay out of this, Ambrose," Silas snarled, his voice rough with pain. "This is between me and Ranger."

Still, Ambrose did not move, his gaze fixed on the scene before him, a look of shock and confusion on his young face. Silas felt a pang of regret, a small voice in the back of his mind whispering that this was not what he had wanted for his grandson, that he had hoped to leave Ambrose with a legacy of strength and power, not this violent, bloody mess.

Ranger took advantage of Silas's distraction, delivering a powerful blow that sent Silas crashing to the ground. Pain shot through his body, and he struggled to push himself up, his limbs heavy and unresponsive. He could feel the weight of his years pressing down on him, the exhaustion and guilt that had been building up for so long finally taking their toll.

Ranger loomed over him, his face a mask of rage and grief. "You're done, Silas," he said, his voice cold and final. "This is the end of your reign."

Silas felt a surge of panic, a desperate need to hold onto his power, to cling to the only thing that had ever given his life meaning. He had spent his entire life building this family, sacrificing everything for the sake of control, and now, in his final moments, he felt it slipping through his fingers like sand.

He looked up at Ranger, his vision blurring as he struggled to hold onto consciousness. "You think you can just take over?" he rasped, his voice weak. "You'll end up just like me. This family… it's a curse. You'll destroy it, just like I did."

Ranger's face softened, a flicker of sadness passing over his features. "Maybe," he said quietly. "But I'd rather try to rebuild it than let you drag it further into darkness."

Silas felt a wave of despair wash over him, a crushing realization that he had become the very thing he had always hated—his father. He had spent his life trying to escape his father's shadow, to build a legacy that would redeem the Farill name, but in the end, he had only succeeded in repeating the same cycle of violence and betrayal.

As his vision darkened, Silas's last thought was a bitter acknowledgment of the truth he had spent a lifetime denying: he had sacrificed everything for a dream that was as hollow and empty as he was. The legacy he had built, the empire he had fought so hard to maintain, would crumble without him, just as his father's had before him.

And as he slipped into darkness, he could only hope that Ambrose would find a way to break the cycle, to escape the curse of the Farill family and forge his own path.

Chapter 15

Ranger stood in the wreckage of what had been Silas's empire, his victory a hollow ache in his chest as he surveyed the aftermath. Blood had been spilled, the bitter residue of a legacy built on shadows and fear, and yet here he was, the man left standing in its wake. Silas was gone, defeated by his own obsessions, by the very ambition that had once made him unstoppable. Ranger knew that to reshape the family, he would need to address the wounds that had festered for so long, to confront the truth of what Silas's leadership had wrought.

Ambrose stood at Ranger's side, his young face pale, his eyes wide with a mixture of awe and uncertainty. He was at an age where impressions lingered, where memories would shape the man he would become, and Ranger felt the weight of that responsibility settle heavily on his shoulders. Ambrose had witnessed the end of an era, the violent destruction of one man's dream, and now he was left to inherit the ashes.

Ranger knelt beside him, placing a firm, steadying hand on his shoulder. "This is your family now, Ambrose. And it's time we change what that means." The boy nodded, though Ranger could see the questions swirling in his eyes, the confusion and fear that had been planted long before he was even old enough to understand. Ambrose was the new blood of the family, the unbroken line that carried with it the hope of something different, a new path forward.

Silas's final words still echoed in Ranger's mind, a dark reminder of the forces that had shaped him. The notion that the Farill family was cursed, destined to repeat its cycle of violence and betrayal, lingered like a shadow over every decision Ranger now faced. He had grown up in that same shadow, hardened by it, molded into something he had once sworn to resist. But he couldn't let that define him, nor could he allow it to poison Ambrose's future.

In the days that followed, Ranger worked tirelessly to consolidate his power, establishing himself as the undisputed leader of the Farill family. He moved with a purpose that surprised even him, driven not by ambition or bloodlust, but by a desire to break the chains that had bound them all to Silas's vision. The men who had once served Silas now looked to him for guidance, their loyalty tentative yet hopeful, sensing the possibility of change in the air.

He met with them one by one, gauging their intentions, assessing their loyalty. He knew the risks, the inherent dangers of leading a family whose very existence had been fueled by fear and violence. But Ranger's vision was clear: he would create something different, something that could exist outside the narrow, brutal world that Silas had cultivated.

Ambrose's education became Ranger's priority. Each morning, he spent time with the boy, teaching him the history of the family but reframing it, giving him an understanding of the past without glorifying its darker moments. Ambrose absorbed it all, asking questions that mirrored the confusion Ranger himself had felt as a child, growing up in the shadows of men who valued power above all else.

Ranger found himself recounting stories of Leah, her kindness and strength, the way she had seen beyond the bloodlines and alliances to the heart of things. It pained him to speak of her, knowing that Ambrose would never truly know the woman who had given him life, but he wanted her presence to live on, to be a part of the family's new legacy. In Leah, Ranger saw the foundation of something better, a vision that did not hinge on violence but on resilience and compassion.

Yet, as he set about reshaping the Farill family, Ranger was constantly reminded of the dangers that still lurked on the periphery. Rival clans, sensing the change in leadership, had already begun probing for weaknesses, testing the strength of the new regime. Ranger met their advances with a calculated resistance, determined not to let them exploit the family's vulnerabilities. He knew that to survive, he would still need to wield the iron fist that Silas had honed, but he promised himself he would temper it with reason, with restraint.

At times, Ranger found himself questioning his own motives, wondering if he was truly capable of changing the family's course or if he was simply delaying the inevitable descent back into darkness. The weight of Silas's legacy bore down on him like an unseen force, a constant reminder of the path that had been carved out before him. He couldn't shake the feeling that he was merely repeating history, that his desire for change was futile in the face of the family's entrenched values.

Ambrose, however, offered a glimmer of hope. The boy had inherited his mother's strength, her resilience, and Ranger clung to that as a lifeline, a reminder that change was possible. He saw in Ambrose a future that was not dictated by fear or violence, a chance to break the cycle that had ensnared the family for generations.

One evening, as Ranger and Ambrose sat in Silas's old study, the boy looked up at him with a question that cut through Ranger's resolve like a knife. "Why did Grandpa want things to be this way? Why did he have to hurt people?"

The question stilled Ranger, the weight of it pressing down on him like an iron shackle. He struggled for an answer, sifting through the memories of his time with Silas, the conversations, the lessons he had learned in blood and betrayal. "He believed he was protecting us," Ranger said at last, choosing his words carefully. "He thought that strength was the only way to keep our family safe. But he was wrong."

Ambrose looked at him with wide, unblinking eyes, his expression solemn. "Then we don't have to be like him," he said, as if it were the simplest truth in the world. The boy's words struck Ranger with a force he hadn't expected, a surge of hope that felt foreign, almost dangerous in its optimism.

Ranger nodded, his resolve hardening. "No, Ambrose. We don't have to be like him."

Yet, even as he spoke those words, Ranger knew the truth was far more complex, that the legacy Silas had left behind could not simply be erased or forgotten. The family's power was rooted in violence, its foundations built on the sacrifices of those who had come before. To lead the Farill family was to walk a razor's edge, to balance the demands of loyalty and strength with the desire for something better.

The months that followed were filled with challenges, with rival clans testing Ranger's resolve, probing for any sign of weakness. Ranger met them with a calculated fury, reminding them that while Silas's reign had ended, the family's strength had not. He refused to let them see any cracks in the armor, knowing that any display of weakness would be exploited.

However, with each victory, with each successful defense of the family's power, Ranger felt the weight of his promise to Ambrose pressing down on him. He was determined to create a different legacy for the boy, to break free from the cycle of violence and betrayal, but he could not ignore the reality of their world, the dangers that lurked at every turn.

And so Ranger continued his delicate dance, a man caught between two worlds, striving to honor the promise he had made to himself and to Ambrose, while navigating the brutal realities of the life they had inherited. He knew the path ahead would be treacherous, filled with obstacles and sacrifices, but he was resolved to see it through, to forge a new future for the family that was not bound by the darkness of its past.

In quiet moments, Ranger would sit alone, his thoughts drifting back to Silas, to the man who had shaped him, for better or worse. He felt a pang of pity for Silas, a sadness for the man who had been consumed by his own ambition, his own fear of weakness. Silas had been a product of his own making, a man who had sacrificed everything for power, only to find himself trapped in a cage of his own design.

Ranger vowed to break free of that cage, to carve out a new path that was not dictated by fear or betrayal. He knew it would not be easy, that the temptations of power and control would always be there, lurking in the shadows, but he was determined to honor the memory of Leah, to create a legacy that would be worthy of the family she had believed in.

As he looked into Ambrose's eyes, Ranger saw the future of the Farill family—a future that held the promise of something different, something better. And for the first time in his life, he felt a glimmer of hope, a belief that perhaps, just perhaps, the cycle could be broken.

He rose from his chair, his gaze steady as he looked out over the Farill estate, the empire that Silas had built and that he now held in his hands. It was a heavy burden, a daunting responsibility, but Ranger was ready to face it. For Ambrose, for Leah, and for the future of the family, he would do whatever it took to change the course of their legacy.

And as the sun dipped below the horizon, casting a golden glow over the estate, Ranger felt a quiet resolve settle over him, a determination to build something new from the ashes of the past.

The road ahead would be fraught with challenges, but he was ready, and he knew that with Ambrose by his side, they could weather whatever storms lay ahead. The Farill family's story was far from over, but for the first time, it held the promise of a brighter tomorrow.

Chapter 16

From the day Ranger took over, it was clear that a new order had come to the Farill family. Under his leadership, there was no denying that changes were being made, though the echoes of the past still held strong. Silas had run the family with an iron fist, a violent, unyielding authority that had cast a long shadow over everyone involved, shaping them in ways they were often unaware of until it was too late. Ranger wanted to distance himself from that—wanted to leave behind a different legacy, one marked by progress rather than the fierce, unrelenting hunger for control that had characterized Silas's reign.

Ranger sat at the head of the long, polished oak table in the Farill estate's grand dining hall, the family's lieutenants gathered around him. It was the first formal meeting he'd called since Silas's death, and the weight of his new role was unmistakable. Some of the older family members still looked at him with wary eyes, a reminder of their loyalty to Silas, but Ranger commanded their respect with a steady resolve that brooked no dissent. He was clear-eyed and calm, a sharp contrast to the way Silas had once held court, and his demeanor had its own kind of gravity.

Over the weeks, he had implemented changes that were both tactical and symbolic. Where Silas had valued aggression above all else, Ranger pushed for strategy and restraint. He limited their operations to fewer, more profitable ventures, moving away from the bloodier enterprises that had once been the family's bread and butter. It was a subtle shift, but it sent a message to those under his command, and to their rivals as well. Ranger's Farill family was different—more calculating, less willing to get their hands dirty unless the reward was undeniable.

Yet, despite his efforts to reframe the family's operations, Ranger could feel the weight of the past pressing down on him, a constant reminder that some things were harder to change than others. The older members of the family seemed content to let him lead, but the old loyalties, the old habits, ran deep. He saw it in their eyes when they spoke of expanding their territories or eliminating a rival who had crossed them; he could feel their silent judgments in every meeting. Ranger's leadership was stable, but it was built on a bedrock that was just waiting for any sign of weakness.

As much as Ranger wanted to step away from the violent legacy Silas had left him, he knew that some traditions could not be ignored. He could not afford to show weakness, not yet, and as much as he loathed it, he found himself making concessions to the old ways. A few of the more violent practices remained intact, remnants of the past he was trying to reshape, yet needing to preserve in some form. Ranger told himself it was temporary, a necessary evil until he could solidify his power and introduce true change.

It was Ambrose, however, who truly tested Ranger's resolve. The boy was growing up fast, an intelligent, perceptive child who absorbed everything around him. Ranger had spent long hours with him, teaching him about the world, about loyalty, about family, and instilling in him a sense of compassion that he hoped would serve as a foundation for the future. But Ambrose was a Farill, and there were certain traits that seemed to be woven into his very being.

Ranger noticed it in small ways at first, the way Ambrose watched people with a calculating gaze, his keen eyes missing nothing, much like his grandfather's had. When Ambrose spoke of family loyalty, there was an intensity in his tone that unnerved Ranger, a glimmer of something darker, something that reminded him far too much of Silas. Ambrose was a boy who, even at his young age, seemed to understand the power dynamics of the family, who was acutely aware of what it meant to be a Farill.

As Ambrose grew older, Ranger found himself haunted by memories of Silas, the echoes of his father-in-law's relentless ambition coloring every interaction with his son. It was a strange, disorienting experience, seeing Silas reflected in the boy's mannerisms, in his curiosity about the family's history, in the way he asked questions that were far too mature for his age. Ranger had hoped that he could shape Ambrose differently, but the family legacy was like a dark undercurrent, drawing Ambrose closer to the very things Ranger had tried to shield him from.

One evening, as they sat together in Ranger's study, Ambrose looked up at him with a seriousness that caught him off guard. "Why don't we expand our reach, Father?" he asked, his tone calm but insistent. "Other families are pushing into our territory. Shouldn't we remind them who the Farills are?"

Ranger paused, studying his son's expression, a sinking feeling settling in his chest. Ambrose's words were not those of a child but of someone who understood the realities of their world, who had inherited the ruthless pragmatism that had defined the Farill family for generations. It was a glimpse of what Ambrose might become, and it terrified Ranger more than he cared to admit.

"Sometimes strength isn't about how far you can reach, Ambrose," Ranger replied carefully, weighing his words. "It's about knowing when to stand firm and when to let things be. Power doesn't always mean taking more. Sometimes it means being smart with what you already have."

Ambrose's brow furrowed, his young mind working through Ranger's response, but the look in his eyes suggested he wasn't entirely convinced. He nodded, seemingly accepting the answer, but Ranger could tell that the boy's curiosity would not be easily sated. Ambrose was a Farill through and through, and he would not simply accept things as they were. The boy had an inquisitive nature, a relentless desire for answers, and Ranger knew that someday soon, Ambrose would start to question the choices he had made, the changes he had tried to bring to the family.

As the days went by, Ranger could feel his grip on the family slipping, a subtle shift that was barely perceptible yet undeniable.

The older lieutenants still deferred to him, but their loyalty was increasingly conditional, tied to his ability to maintain the family's strength. Ranger had introduced reforms, yes, but he could see that the family's underlying nature resisted those changes, that they clung to the old ways with a tenacity that defied reason. They were still Farills, and for them, power and violence were inseparable.

It was during a particularly tense meeting with his lieutenants that Ranger realized just how deeply entrenched those loyalties were. One of the older men, a grizzled veteran who had served Silas loyally for decades, spoke up, his tone respectful but firm. "With respect, sir, we've noticed some... changes in the way things are run. Some of us wonder if we're losing sight of what made the Farills strong in the first place."

The statement hung in the air, a silent challenge that Ranger could not ignore. He knew what the man was implying—that his leadership was seen as softer, less ruthless than Silas's, and that some of the family's older members viewed this as a weakness. It was a subtle reminder of the precarious position he held, a position that required a careful balance between reform and tradition.

Ranger met the man's gaze, his expression hardening. "Strength doesn't come from bloodshed alone," he said evenly. "Silas taught us that, yes, but there's more to power than fear. We have resources, alliances, influence that extends beyond violence. My goal is to ensure the Farill family endures, not just survives."

The man nodded, his expression neutral, but Ranger could see the doubt lingering in his eyes. He knew that it would take more than words to convince the family's old guard, that they would need to see proof that his way could work. And even as he spoke, Ranger felt the weight of Silas's legacy bearing down on him, a dark, unshakable presence that seemed to defy his every attempt at change.

That night, as Ranger watched Ambrose sleeping in his bed, he was struck by the enormity of what he had taken on. Silas had believed that power was a weapon, a tool to be wielded with ruthless precision, and Ranger had inherited that legacy, whether he wanted it or not. But he could not shake the feeling that he was merely delaying the inevitable, that Ambrose, too, would grow into the same darkness that had claimed Silas.

Ranger had once believed that he could break the cycle, that he could carve out a new path for the family, one that was not bound by violence and betrayal. But the reality of his position, the resistance he faced at every turn, suggested otherwise. The Farill family was like a living entity, its identity woven into the lives of everyone connected to it, and Ranger could see that his efforts at change were like ripples in a vast, unyielding ocean.

Ambrose stirred in his sleep, and Ranger's heart tightened with a mixture of hope and dread. He wanted a different life for his son, a life free from the shadows that had haunted their family for generations. But as he looked at Ambrose's peaceful face, he couldn't escape the gnawing doubt that perhaps, despite his best efforts, the boy was already bound to the same fate.

Ranger leaned over, brushing a hand gently across Ambrose's forehead, his resolve hardening. He would keep trying, he told himself. He would do whatever it took to ensure that Ambrose did not fall into the same darkness that had claimed Silas. Yet, as he left the room, he couldn't shake the haunting feeling that the past was not so easily escaped, that the legacy Silas had left behind would continue to shape them all, whether they liked it or not.

Chapter 17

It had been months since Silas's death, yet his memory lingered in every corner of the Farill estate, a quiet but unrelenting reminder of the brutal legacy he had left behind. For Ranger, the weight of that memory seemed to press harder with each passing day. Silas's methods, his iron-fisted control, the cold calculations that guided his every action—they haunted Ranger like an invisible tether, binding him to a path he had tried so desperately to deviate from. Yet, no matter how he struggled to reshape the family, there was an insidious resistance within it, a force that held tight to the old ways, as if the spirit of Silas himself were holding them all hostage to his ruthless vision.

Ranger had always believed that by taking over, he could right Silas's wrongs, steer the family toward a less bloody future. But he couldn't deny that, in his pursuit of that vision, he had sacrificed parts of himself. The lines he had once drawn in the sand—lines that set him apart from Silas—had slowly eroded over time, worn down by the necessity of survival, by the constant, unyielding demand for strength. Ranger had once vowed to break the cycle of violence, but as he looked at the choices he'd made, the lengths he'd gone to secure his position, he wondered if he had merely become another iteration of the very thing he despised.

What weighed most heavily on him, however, was Ambrose. The boy was no longer the child he'd once known, full of innocent questions and eager curiosity. Now, he stood with a sharpness that belied his age, a calculating gaze that often left Ranger unsettled. It was as though Silas's spirit lived on within him, an unrelenting, watchful presence that observed everything, judged everything, missing nothing. And Ranger had watched as Ambrose's influence grew, his words carrying a quiet authority among the family's lieutenants, who spoke of him with a mix of respect and cautious admiration.

Ranger could sense the change most acutely in the way Ambrose interacted with him. The boy was no longer content to follow instructions or accept Ranger's guidance without question. He had grown assertive, bolder in his opinions, unafraid to voice his own ideas about how the family should be run. One evening, they sat alone in Ranger's study, a thick silence between them that seemed to hum with unspoken thoughts. Ambrose leaned back, his expression calm but unyielding.

"Father," he began, his voice measured, "I've been thinking about our reach, the way we've scaled back operations. It seems… inefficient."

Ranger studied him, noting the keen intelligence in his son's gaze, the glint of ambition that reminded him all too painfully of Silas.

"Efficiency isn't always about reaching further, Ambrose," Ranger replied cautiously. "Sometimes it's about keeping what we have, holding it tightly, and knowing that our strength doesn't come from expanding but from stability."

Ambrose nodded thoughtfully, but Ranger could see that his answer hadn't landed, hadn't resonated the way he'd hoped. Ambrose's gaze drifted across the room, his eyes lingering on the portrait of Silas that hung on the wall behind them, his expression contemplative.

"But isn't strength also about commanding respect?" Ambrose asked, his tone almost philosophical. "I think sometimes we lose that when we don't show others what we're capable of."

Ranger held back a sigh, feeling the growing distance between them with each passing word. Silas's shadow stretched between them, an unbreakable barrier that seemed to drive Ambrose toward the very legacy Ranger had fought to escape. The boy admired his grandfather, revered him in a way that unsettled Ranger, for Silas's ruthless vision seemed to call to Ambrose, shaping him in ways Ranger couldn't prevent.

As the weeks went by, Ranger found himself torn between pride and dread as Ambrose continued to make strides within the family. The boy had an instinctive understanding of power, a natural charisma that drew people to him, and he wielded it with a quiet assurance that belied his youth. Ranger could see the family's lieutenants gravitating toward Ambrose, their loyalty slowly transferring from father to son as they recognized in him the traits they had once revered in Silas. Ambrose was becoming the leader they respected, the one who spoke of the Farill family's legacy with a fierce pride that reminded them of the days when Silas ruled with an unyielding hand.

It was this very loyalty that both reassured and frightened Ranger, for he knew all too well where such loyalty led. He had seen it in Silas's eyes, felt its weight in his own decisions, and he feared that Ambrose would one day face the same choice—the choice to sacrifice everything for the sake of power, to trade compassion for control.

One evening, as Ranger sat alone in the quiet of his study, he was struck by a memory, a fleeting image of Silas sitting in this very chair, his face hard and unyielding as he spoke of the family's legacy. Ranger remembered the cold resolve in Silas's eyes, the ruthless determination that had defined every action, every decision. And he felt a chill run through him as he realized that he was now faced with the same dilemma Silas had once faced, the same choice between loyalty to family and loyalty to his vision of what the family could be.

The following day, Ranger watched Ambrose speaking with some of the family's older members, his voice steady and confident as he discussed the family's future. There was a calmness to him, a natural ease that reminded Ranger painfully of Silas. But there was also something darker, a quiet intensity that suggested he was not above using the same brutal methods his grandfather had once wielded without hesitation.

As Ranger listened, he felt a pang of regret, a sense that he had somehow failed in his efforts to protect Ambrose from the cycle of violence and betrayal that had defined the Farill family for generations. He had tried to give the boy a different path, a life free from the weight of the family's bloody history, but it seemed that no matter what he did, the past had a way of asserting itself, a relentless force that pulled them all back into its orbit.

In the weeks that followed, Ranger found himself growing increasingly isolated, his influence within the family waning as Ambrose's star continued to rise. He watched from a distance as his son navigated the world of power and politics with a natural ease, his every action a reminder of the legacy Ranger had tried so hard to escape. It was as though Silas's spirit had found a new vessel, a new heir to carry on his vision of the family, and Ranger felt a deep, inescapable sorrow as he realized that he was powerless to stop it.

Late one night, as Ranger sat alone in the darkness of his study, he felt the weight of Silas's memory pressing down on him, a heavy, unrelenting presence that seemed to mock his every effort to escape its grasp. He thought of the promises he had made, the dreams he had once held for a different future, and he felt a pang of regret, a sense that he had somehow failed to live up to his own ideals.

However, as he looked around the room, his gaze lingering on the portrait of Silas that hung on the wall, he realized that perhaps his struggle had never been about escaping the past, but about learning to live with it. He had inherited a legacy of blood and betrayal, a history steeped in violence, and while he had tried to change it, he now understood that some things could not be so easily erased.

In that moment, Ranger felt a quiet resolve settle over him, a sense that he could still make a difference, that he could still guide

Ambrose toward a future that was not defined by the past. He would not abandon his son to the same darkness that had claimed Silas, would not allow him to become a mere echo of a man who had been consumed by his own ambition.

Rising from his chair, Ranger made his way to Ambrose's room, pausing for a moment outside the door as he gathered his thoughts. He knew that the road ahead would not be easy, that Ambrose would resist him, that the boy would cling to the ideals and beliefs that had been instilled in him from a young age. But Ranger was determined to try, to fight for the future he had once dreamed of, even if it meant standing against his own son.

As he pushed open the door, he felt a strange sense of peace, a calmness that belied the challenges that lay ahead. He knew that he was stepping into a battle that might never truly be won, a struggle that would test his every resolve, but he was ready. The ghosts of the past still lingered, their shadows stretching across his path, but Ranger was determined to move forward, to forge a new legacy, one that would finally put Silas's spirit to rest.

Because for all his flaws, all his mistakes, Ranger still believed in a future where the Farill family could break free from the chains of its own history, where Ambrose could grow into a man who did not carry the weight of his grandfather's sins. It was a vision that seemed almost impossible, a dream that had been all but shattered by the harsh realities of the world they lived in, but Ranger clung to it with a quiet, unyielding determination.

For as long as he had breath in his body, he would fight for that future, he would defy the ghosts of the past and forge a new path, a path that would finally set them free.

Chapter 18

The long journey of the Farill family, its blood-soaked history, and relentless cycles of violence had finally come to this moment. Ranger stood at the edge of a new era, watching as Ambrose took his place as the leader of the family. The room was filled with familiar faces, most showing thinly veiled excitement and cautious respect as Ambrose held court, issuing commands with the ease of a seasoned leader.

Ambrose was no longer the boy Ranger had once known, the boy he had hoped to shield from this world. He was a Farill through and through, and as he surveyed the room, his piercing gaze had the cold detachment Ranger remembered all too well from Silas's reign. This was the Farill legacy: power and fear forged into a weapon of control. Ranger could only watch as his son, grown and ruthless, fell seamlessly into the role of a leader, his resolve unmoved by any whispers of mercy.

Ranger felt himself slipping into a quiet, reflective state, a detached calm. There was nothing more he could do. The fate of the family was in Ambrose's hands now, and whatever future lay ahead was shaped by forces he had long fought but never fully understood. He could sense in Ambrose an ambition sharper than his own, sharper even than Silas's—a hunger to rise above and become a name that would echo beyond even the borders of their empire. Ambrose held a charisma that commanded respect without a word, a demeanor that brokered no argument. His was a cool, calculating ruthlessness that was terrifying in its simplicity.

The room stilled as Ambrose spoke, his voice carrying a confidence beyond his years. "We've seen other families come and go, vying for power only to fall by our hands. The Farill name, our empire, is built on more than power alone. It's built on resilience. From today forward, we set our sights higher—beyond petty rivalry, beyond the usual games." His eyes flashed with a look Ranger recognized: the vision of someone who saw the world as his for the taking.

Ranger felt a pang of regret. All those years spent trying to change the future of this family, all the sacrifices, the betrayals, had led him to this. Had he been naïve to think he could shield Ambrose from this life, this inevitable turn toward power and control? He remembered his younger self, convinced he could break free from Silas's influence, reshape the family, turn their legacy into something different. Now, Ambrose was the image of that lost dream—a ruthless Farill leader, bearing the weight of a history that Ranger had tried and failed to alter.

Ambrose dismissed the gathered lieutenants with a subtle wave, and the room emptied, leaving Ranger and his son alone in silence. There was a coldness to the room that stung at Ranger's resolve, a reminder that this was no longer his realm. He had lost any influence he once held; the mantle had passed, and with it, any hope he had clung to for a different life. Ambrose's eyes found his, and for the first time, Ranger saw something in them that chilled him to the bone—a darkness, an unyielding certainty that reminded him of Silas, yes, but somehow more refined, more dangerously focused.

"You wanted this, didn't you?" Ranger finally spoke, his voice a weary whisper. "You wanted this from the beginning."

Ambrose's face betrayed nothing. "I wanted to make things right, to make things better. You taught me that. You wanted the family to rise above, didn't you?"

The question lingered, painfully familiar. Silas had often asked questions with the same slippery conviction, as if challenging Ranger to admit to desires he didn't even realize he had. But Ambrose's gaze was far colder than Silas's ever had been.

"Yes," Ranger admitted softly. "I wanted something better, but I didn't want it to cost us everything."

Ambrose tilted his head, a faint smile curving his lips. "Everything has a cost, Father. The family doesn't rise without sacrifice."

The words felt like a verdict, a final declaration that erased any illusions Ranger might have harbored. Ambrose was no innocent stepping into the family business—he was a man who understood fully what power demanded, and he had chosen his path with chilling clarity. Ranger felt a coldness settle in his chest as he realized the truth. The history he had tried so hard to escape had repeated itself, even more violently than before.

Ambrose turned his gaze out the window, as if already envisioning the future he intended to claim. "The other families will know soon enough that the Farill legacy is still strong, still iron-clad," he said, his voice distant. "But we won't make the same mistakes. We'll be smarter, more cautious. We'll reach farther, but with purpose."

Ranger could barely bring himself to respond. He had once dreamed of this, of a family that rose above its own violent tendencies, that could walk away from bloodshed and fear. But Ambrose's words, his intentions, were a stark reminder of the truth that Ranger had always feared: the family was bound to its own history, inextricably tied to violence and betrayal.

The quiet realization brought him no comfort, only the grim acceptance that his own efforts had merely paved the way for Ambrose's ambitions. Ranger felt the weight of his father's ghost settle over him, as if Silas himself were watching, vindicated.

Ambrose finally looked back at him, his gaze sharp and unyielding. "Father, you taught me a great deal—more than you may realize. You taught me that power is not in loyalty or even in love. Power is in legacy. The Farill name carries that legacy, and I intend to make it stronger than ever."

Ranger swallowed the bitterness rising in his throat. His son was no longer his; he was a product of the legacy Ranger had tried to deny, shaped by the very darkness he had once hoped to escape. He had wanted Ambrose to be different, but he had only created a stronger, colder version of Silas—a man bound to a fate he couldn't outrun.

As Ambrose turned and left, leaving Ranger alone in the silence, Ranger felt a strange sense of finality, as though the family had already sealed its fate. Silas had once spoken of legacy with a kind of blind devotion, a relentless drive to build something indestructible. And now, Ambrose carried that vision forward, determined to expand the Farill family's reach, driven by the same ruthless ambition that had claimed Silas and now claimed Ranger.

In the quiet of the room, the echoes of the past loomed large, the ghosts of those who had come before watching with silent approval. Ranger's thoughts drifted back to a time long ago, to a young man who had once dreamed of a different path, a life free from the chains of power and control. But that young man was gone, lost to the unyielding demands of legacy, a history he had tried and failed to rewrite.

As he sat there, the words of his father's final warning echoed in his mind, a prophecy he had never believed, now realized in the form of his son. History repeats if we don't learn why events happened before. But if we know, we can change it. We can change it and make it too the best to ourselves.

Afterword

Writing the *A first... series* has been a journey into the darkest corners of ambition, power, and the human heart. As I brought Silas, Ranger, and Ambrose to life, I wanted to explore the magnetic allure and devastating consequences of loyalty and legacy, and how they shape not only individuals but entire generations. Each character's story is not merely about family ties or mafia politics; it's about the inherent struggle within all of us—to overcome or succumb to the forces that shape our destinies.

Silas, Ranger, and Ambrose all carry pieces of their family's legacy, but they also wrestle with their own dreams, regrets, and desires. At their core, each man struggles with a profound need for control, for the ability to rise above and escape the pitfalls of those who came before him. In Silas, we see an unrelenting pursuit of power that slowly chips away at his humanity. Ranger brings a glimmer of hope—a possibility that perhaps, this time, things might be different. And yet, as Ambrose steps forward, there's an unsettling realization that history, once set in motion, is incredibly hard to stop.

Writing the story of the Farill family meant reflecting on how cycles of violence, betrayal, and ambition are so difficult to break, especially when they are embedded in the traditions we inherit. The legacy we leave—whether by choice or circumstance—is an inevitable part of us, but we are also capable of reshaping it, of making decisions that can steer it in a new direction. This duality, this tension between destiny and free will, has been at the heart of the story.

I hope this book has allowed you, the reader, to consider your own legacies—the influences, traditions, and histories that shape you—and to wonder what it takes to truly break free from the patterns we inherit. While *A first...* may be a story set within the world of a crime family, the questions it raises are universal: What are we willing to sacrifice to secure our futures? How do we escape becoming the very thing we despise? And is redemption possible when we acknowledge the ghosts that haunt us?

Thank you for taking this journey with me, for stepping into the complex, often brutal world of the Farill family. I hope you've found their story as challenging and compelling as I have in writing it. The story of Silas, Ranger, and Ambrose may end here, but the questions their lives raise about legacy, family, and ambition will live on, just as their memories will linger in the shadows of every reader who comes across them.

Your L.H. Kuhrau